Nagini
Anarchy

Nagini Anarchy

A Novel from The Chai House

Priti Srivastava

This book is dedicated to the way. For you, I practice not doing; like water, pani, jal, jeevan, I shall nourish & be nourished, satisfied with the places others may consider too low, including me. A streaming reminder to let go of control, to follow a simple path, to be present, like you I hope to one day flow.

Contents

1: Then

Ana sat patiently, waiting for her interview to begin. She had prepared as much as possible, all that was left now was to actually meet with her potential new boss. She looked over to the empty workstation and imagined sitting there, shadowing in her new role, maybe even as soon as this Monday, which meant Ana would have money in her bank account in two weeks. Her parents' life insurance was sitting safely in the bank, an electronic number which she checked every day when she called the bank, it rising just slightly but still more than she ever imagined making in her entire lifetime. She had no desire to touch the funds, Ammi and Papa would want her to use it on college or helping others, not paying for a lifestyle she could not afford because she refused to get a job.

Ana wished she didn't have the money. She would have given anything to not be an orphan. This was a term she used for herself, only to herself. She knew that claiming to be orphaned at the age of nineteen looked pathetic, so she kept it a secret. She did feel pathetic.

Her parents' coworkers had stopped calling, checking in, just days after the accident. Ana felt so alone in the world. She didn't know how to navigate it and reminded herself her parents did not know how to navigate living in a new country. But at least they had had each other. There was no one for her.

She wished she could have talked with Ammi this morning. Her biggest fans; Ammi and Papa had believed their daughter could achieve any goal she set her mind to. Ana's heart sank a little when she remembered that she wouldn't need to be interviewing for this job if she could still talk to Ammi. She would still be at university.

Ana brushed her sadness away and picked up the newspaper that had been left for visitors. Maybe that included her, maybe it didn't. She did not care; she needed something to distract herself. There was a pile of newspapers on the desk she assumed would be hers to clean up if she was lucky enough to get the job. It would make sense that the Chief Executive Officer of Willard's Wellness Waters would leave the task of bundling old newspapers and arranging pickup for recycling to his next assistant.

She picked up the fresh edition that had been left for Mr. Paisley's visitors and flipped through the pages. She stopped to read the Local section of that day's *Gazette*, the color photo of a large black bobcat catching her attention. The story focused on how the bobcat population was in great danger of going extinct and biologists had placed a tracker on the black bobcat, who was the feature photo. Ana admired the wildlife photography and chuckled to herself when she saw the biologists had named him Rufus. Ammi had read her so many stories of Saaya, so as far as Ana was concerned, all black kitties reminded her of them. Of course, Saaya was for children and they never ran into the problems the poor bobcat in the photo had. Rufus was a melanistic bobcat, extremely rare and, for that reason, sought after by poachers for his coat. The biologists hoped that by tracking Rufus, they could determine his range, habitat, and how many female bobcats Rufus may meet to breed with. Four kittens a year didn't seem like much, but the biologists estimated Rufus' age to be three, meaning he could end up fathering forty kittens; greatly helping their declining numbers.

Ana flipped through the local section to the classifieds. She made sure to push past the want ads, so she did not look rude (just in case her interviewer stepped out) and stopped to read a large advertisement the state had taken. The black-and-white image of a man with money bags didn't quite match what they were advertising; the state was offering bounties for the capture of Rock Rattlesnakes - fifty cents for adults and ten cents for juveniles. Ana rolled her eyes and then glanced around to make sure she was still alone in the reception area.

Her parents had discussed this many times, most snakes, including rattlesnakes, rarely bothered humans, but the natural human reaction was to kill them, not even because they were venomous but simply because snakes were weird to humans. Unknown and unpredictable. Her parents had told her a similar program had been implemented in India, where they had grown up. Villagers captured and bred the Indian Python, turning in the dead snakes to the British for a reliable source of income; releasing an equal number of young snakes back to the wild to offset the killing they did. Her parents were herpetologists, and had warned her of this program, especially when it came to the future of rattlesnakes and the food chain.

"It's all connected," Ammi used to say. Ana knew what her mother meant but at the same time, did not quite understand.

Ana quickly folded the newspaper up as she heard voices behind the door of the office. She smoothed down her skirt and crossed her ankles, an attempt to sit properly, how she had learned from Madame Manners, the advice column for women that ran in the *Gazette*. The door to the office opened and two men stood in the doorway, exchanging pleasantries. Ana could tell by their interaction that the taller man, with a head full of mahogany brown hair was the person who might be her future boss. The shorter man with sandy blonde hair shook the taller man's hand and laughed before exiting.

"You'll have your hands full with this one!" the shorter man said, and Ana did not know what to say, she stuck frozen by his striking blue eyes, one of which he winked at her.

"Ana?" the taller man began, before gesturing to himself, "Willard Paisley. Welcome to WWW, please join me, c'mon step inside."

Ana smiled at Mr. Paisley and said hello before stepping into his enormous office. She stood waiting to be told where to sit; there were chairs in front of his large desk as well as a sofa and two lounge chairs. Ana watched as Mr. Paisley settled into the large chair behind his even larger desk and then sat in the chair across from him.

"So, Ana, what an interesting last name! I hope it doesn't mean anything about your attitude! Where exactly are you from?"

"Ahh-naa, it's a nickname," Ana corrected Mr. Paisley's enunciation before answering, "I'm from the city."

"Yeah, I saw on your cover letter. I could never pronounce that. You know what I mean *Ahh-nnaa*, where are you *really* from?"

2: When

"You look amazing."

Prem turned around and saw Riley peeking at her through their kitchen.

"I'm so nervous!" Prem babbled as she applied her lip gloss in the mirror.

Prem smiled at Riley through the reflection as she watched her roommate, her best friend, her *everything* approaching to adjust her outfit. After so many years of being single, Prem felt so warm in her heart whenever Riley's arms wrapped around her waist; Prem had never realized how deprived of affection she had been. She loved feeling so close to Riley and vowed to never complain about having to touch up her makeup after Riley pecked kisses on Prem's cheeks and neck, their bodies slightly coiled when Prem reached back with her arms to return the affection, playfully grabbing Riley's ass.

"You've got this," Riley affirmed, holding Prem's gaze in the mirror, Riley's chin resting on Prem's shoulder.

"I've got this? More like I've really missed this," Prem concluded before fully turning around and giving Riley a light smooch on the lips, careful not to smudge her sticky lip gloss.

"Missed getting ready in the morning? Or having to set an alarm clock? Why?" Riley joked.

"Absolutely, I've missed both. Because I actually *like* being a productive member of society," Prem replied, laughing, "It feels so good to actually be going out in the field, actually interviewing, not just copy-editing or fact checking someone else's work. I'll be a storyteller again! And having the *Gazette* on my resume is going to look so good, it's not just that they are paying me! By the way, my lip gloss looks great on you, Riley."

Riley jokingly puckered her lips in the mirror, striking a pose like a supermodel before wiping off Prem's candy scented, luxury brand, magenta lip gloss. "Y'know, if I was you, I would have taken advantage of being able to sleep in every day for as long as I possibly could. Who cares about being a productive member of society? What does that even mean, Prem? And I mean, think about me, I did love coming home to dinner on the table and a clean apartment every night. I am *really* going to miss that," Riley joked with mock sorrow.

"Gender roles!" Prem acted shocked as she admonished Riley, giving Riley's shoulder a playful tap with her open palm, "You know that I think staying home is only fun for a few days. I get bored too easily. And am I really supposed to take career advice from someone who tells their patients, 'Do the least amount of work that you have to do to not get fired?'"

"Don't give me that look! You know I'm right! No workplace is going to even send a counselor in if one of their employees dies! Most of us spend more time at work than with our loved ones! Don't give them more than you have to!" Riley retorted.

"Ok, I know I sound crazy to you, but I *actually* give a shit; I just don't know how to relax, and I'll eventually get used to it. I'm okay with that," Prem continued sincerely, "I do appreciate you supporting me the past three months Riley. The competition is so fierce and there's just so many more experienced journalists living here. I still think I only I booked this one because we're both Brown. That's the only reason Heath contacted me, although neither of us are actually *from* India…"

"Okay, enough. We've had this discussion, but we can keep having it if you want Prem. First, as I've told you again and again, you don't have to thank me for loving you. And second, yeah, plenty of people are going to think you know someone *they* know just cause you're both Indian. It's not like Heath cold called you, Amelia gave him your name, that's how people get jobs. It's totally normal. You're not the only one who suffers from assumptions, you know I've dealt with that a little, it isn't like those updates to the DSM happened a long time ago. My peers, my attendings, you've heard *all* the stories. Well, most of them," Riley sighed.

"And I hope you keep telling me all the stories. I love you, Riley. Forever and ever," Prem pledged.

Prem rushed to finish getting ready, Riley tapping her toes in mock annoyance at having to wait while Prem moisturized every centimeter of skin. "Babe, you do not want to know what happens if I do not apply this liberally," Prem half joked as she held up her expensive prescription moisturizer. Riley hadn't seen Prem at her worst yet. They hadn't had a cold, dry winter together; Prem rushing to take a quick and cold shower each morning so her skin didn't dry out and begin flaking off in scales. Prem closed her eyes and thanked the creator for dermatologists and their healing salves before rushing to pack up her things. She wanted to make sure she got Riley to the hospital on time; there was nothing worse than someone doing you a favor but causing them extra work. Prem *never* wanted to be that person to Riley. She had looked for this type of love for so long, not even believing it was real, much less possible for her. Prem wasn't sure if she could keep on living if she ever took Riley, the woman she loved, for granted.

3: When

After Prem dropped Riley off at the hospital, she played a game, imagining she was a professional driver, hyping herself up to make up for the fact that she rarely drove. Her issue with driving was that she had to trust the other humans on the road. She didn't want to trust the other drivers on the road, but in this one way she was willing to give up control. Being a passenger was tough for Prem and driving was even tougher.

As she made her way to the location of the interview, Prem pretended she drove a truck every day for her job, delivering produce to all the area markets, telling herself this journey was no big deal and there was an expert behind the wheel. An expert used to dealing with drivers on the road who *weren't* professionals. Trusting her own skills so she could trust theirs. She got into the mindset of this character, smiling as she imagined a delivery driver who loved her job would. A true professional was expertly driving Riley's pickup truck to Prem's interview with Manasa in Mirror Marsh. She wavered as she thought back to when she had last taken this turn towards Hell's Hill. This past weekend was her first time having driven down this unpaved road, it was special taking this route for the first time with Riley in the passenger seat as her co-pilot, practicing so she felt comfortable, so she knew how much time the drive would take, and to be aware of any road closures or other delays to prepare for today's interview. She would never forget how Riley supported her, didn't think it was a waste of time to drive out to Mirror Marsh just to practice driving the truck. It was a big deal for Prem, she hadn't learned how to drive until just a few years ago and so rarely left the city. She loved the feeling of snaking her way through the crowd when the crosswalk changed its signal to walk, masses of people hopping on and off public transit with her whenever she needed to get anywhere. During the week at least, she hated how the city reduced schedules over the weekend, it had always been that way, whichever city she had lived in.

Manasa had lived in *the* city for a while, Prem had learned through digging through permits. She had purchased the parcel of land and over time built a very small cottage, living in a trailer soon after she had purchased it, while her cottage and this curious stepwell were built. Prem knew this story wasn't too uncommon, many rich families chose to move to the middle of nowhere, gain privacy by making access to their lives difficult. Yes, Mirror Marsh was out there, in the middle of nowhere really, but why would someone as young as Manasa want to live in the middle of nowhere by herself? If anything happened, there was no one around to help her.

Prem shuddered as she thought about being stuck in Mirror Marsh at night, Riley had told her how dark it got out here in the middle of nowhere. Riley had been excited when she said it, talking about how the darkness made it so you could see the light from so many more stars in the sky, sometimes even celestial events. Prem pretended to be excited at that, nodding at Riley's suggestion to stay as long as she needed to check them out. She didn't want to be driving these dirt roads after the sun set, much less driving on them in pitch dark silence. Prem could barely see at night and if she got in an accident or ended up with Riley's pickup off the road, it would be not just be embarrassing but a repair she wouldn't be able to afford. Prem was still looking for a consistent paycheck, so it would be on Riley to fix Prem's mistake. And if an accident happened after the interview, it would mean walking for hours in the dark until she got back to the main road. Riley had said there were packs of coyotes out here and even a few bobcats had been sighted. Prem smiled like she knew she was supposed to, feigning excitement at the wildlife of Mirror Marsh as she decided she would have to lie down and die, there was no way she could outrun any of them.

4: Now

Jani stood up from her seat with purpose, it was time to move on from her rest underneath the oak. And as she did every single time she stood, she did so with no use of her upper limbs. This time she hugged her biceps towards her chest, opposite hands forming into the shape of an X across her upper body; the work of this standing movement relying entirely on the strength of her legs. Back in Jani's village, Deer Commons, on repeat she told the Junior Guardians that this one skill was the one they'd never regret practicing. Jani didn't tell them her momma had told her that, how it was a game they had played together, seeing who could stand up with quickness, steadiness, and grace; *look Momma, no hands!*

When she first became Commander of the Guardians, Jani would list off the scenarios where this skill would be beneficial to those she was teaching. If you're held hostage, hands secured behind your back with unbreakable restraints, could you be agile enough to engage in combat with your kicks? What if you're stabbed in your dominant arm and forced to rely on your weak arm to fight? She chuckled to herself as she stood underneath the enormous oak tree; hell, just to be able to surprise people when you fall and get up with no help if you're lucky enough to live to age when your skull is covered in white hair, she used to lecture. Jani rolled an acorn top away with her toe as she thought about how she couldn't wait to be old and prank the youngsters one day in Deer Commons. It would take a long time for them to believe she was so frail she couldn't stand up after a fall, by forcing them to watch their Commander grow weak, she could give them quite a scare! Those were the types of pranks Jani liked best and she almost never got to play them, Hans had taught her she needed to be seen as serious, so she faked it always. Jani tied back her hair and rolled her eyes at the thought of Hans.

Jani kept her favorite part about learning this drill secret for the most immature of JGs. The ones she wanted to make sure stuck with their apprenticeship. She worried about the novice JGs, over the years she had watched how many of them clung to their humor as armor, a few choosing incompetence rather than taking a risk and being told they were no good.

"If you're scared to try this drill with us, you can practice on the toilets, in private, come out, still wash your hands," Jani would say to them after pulling them aside, watching them decide if she was serious, "No one would know."

There had been many moons since she'd taken over as Commander but still each spring Jani knew Hans must be fighting to roll his eyes when she let the JGs know the easiest version of her 'look momma, no hands' drill could be found on the toilet.

Hans didn't find Jani's joke funny, but she no longer took offense. Over the years she learned he found little funny. He had corrected her that first year they were in charge together, told her to treat the boys as professionals so they'd see themselves that way too.

Hans had barely acknowledged her through all their planning for orientation, but had thoughts to give now. Jani unclenched her jaw and spoke, not daring to look at him as she didn't know what her anger would do if she registered his judgement, "They're clearly jokesters. I'd rather I failed them than they failed themselves. They don't have to change to be like me. Plenty of people around here willing to fail 'em and they don't even know it. Like you."

Hans had no reply to that, he had witnessed it first hand many times before that conversation and since. The difference now was things had changed. Hans had grown to *like* Jani's outsider's way of thinking, he liked when Jani surprised him, made him see things he normally couldn't, like that. And Jani had grown to understand Hans' need for structure, for control, for belief. Deer Commons provided safety, as promised, and yet it no longer felt safe for any generation that resided there. Hans was struggling to believe that it could.

They laughed about it now, often when it was late at night and they visited one another on overnight duty. One slipping out of their dorm and the other leaving the door to the Command Station unlocked. Jani had grown up shitting in the Borderlands, weapon in hand. Of course, she got off the toilet without using her hands! One of them would inevitably make the joke as they lay intertwined, dangerously close to being caught, their stomachs cramping from laughing so hard, one time Hans thought he'd need the medics, that Jani wouldn't have time to get dressed. The humiliation that waited no matter which medic arrived.

The thought reminded Jani why she was under the oak and that she had to get moving. She had to watch out for Drishti, having stolen ancient writings from the Scriptorium. The Council had warned Jani that at best she would be racing to give the cultists of Mirror Marsh intel on Deer Commons. At worst, Drishti had been converted, had escaped Deer Commons to complete a ritual at the ancient stone monument rumored to be here. The Council warned Jani that Deer Commons was not prepared for who Drishti might awaken. Who Drishti might bring back to their gates.

Jani kicked the acorn top in anger as she thought of The Council's instructions, not to bring Drishti back to safety but to take care of her. To ensure the safety of Deer Commons. That they had sent her and not Hans, although he held full citizenship, was able to vote, to speak. Jani knew it wasn't a question of loyalty, they just knew for certain what Jani was capable of in the Borderlands.

5: When

Heath, Amelia's roommate's ex-boyfriend and the editor of the *Gazette*, the state's largest daily newspaper, that had reached out to offer Prem this freelance gig, tentatively asking, "Have you met Manasa before?"

Prem had never even heard of the woman and Amelia hadn't given her the heads up that Heath was going to call, but Prem knew exactly who Heath was and what this conversation, this opportunity could mean for her career, so she lied, instantly feeling like a snake but desperate for the chance for an in at the paper with the largest subscriber base in the Midwest, "Yeah, I don't *know* her know her, but like, friends of friends, right?" Prem had giggled, hoping she sounded a little flirtatious and hoping Amelia's roommate wouldn't take it any type of way if she found out. Not too many people ever picked up that Prem was gay. Not too many people thought to think differently than they were used to.

"Oh, thank God! Friends of friends!" Heath exclaimed, "Oh, I am so glad. We have to have this special section on Earth Day and the investors suggested a real feel-good story, what the average man can do to save the planet. In the ideas room this crazy story about the lady building a well in Mirror Marsh came up and weirdly enough, they LOVED it. A real underdog fighting powerful developers for land. But when we reached out to her, Manasa wanted no publicity and refused to be interviewed. She didn't want a bunch of cars and people disturbing the preserve she'd created. We had to pivot and were going to cover a menu for a 'Meatless Month of Meals' and the investors were not too happy about that when they found out." Health paused.

"Advertisers?" Prem guessed.

Prem thought she had put her foot in her mouth when she heard Heath gulp, but then realized he was drinking something after he began coughing.

"Whoa, sorry Prem," Heath held the phone away and Prem imagined he was coughing into the crook of his arm, "Yeah, a little bit of advertising but off the record, seriously, a few of the investors have money in steak and slaughterhouses so encouraging our readership to go veg was just not acceptable to them."

"Of course, you gotta make the bosses happy," Prem conceded, another reminder of why she got canned from the *Only Daily*. Prem promised herself she would do better with this opportunity, if Heath chose her.

"Exactly Prem! I'm so glad you get it," Heath coughed again, Prem waited patiently through his pause to take another sip, "So yeah, some didn't want us to run the story about the benefits of going vegetarian, there were talks with the editors above me and then Manasa called me back! She changed her mind, wanted to go ahead but only with someone who understood or had familiarity with Indian culture and could connect her creation with the stepwells in India, and I promised her I could do it. The editors were so happy with me, like I had anything to do with her changing her mind. I think she wants to get publicity to prevent the dam from being built, like that would ever happen. Thank goodness for Amelia, I wanted to kill her sometimes but because she helped me, I get the credit," Heath chuckled as Prem shifted uncomfortably, she had been leaning against the door frame in the kitchen and then stood on both feet when he made that comment, Heath never noticing his rudeness, just continuing, "but she knew you! *Oh, you gotta talk to my friend Prem!*" Heath mocking Amelia's southern accent in a falsetto before returning to his own voice, "Let me give you the scoop and then you can tell me if you want the gig."

Prem played the game, told him it was likely, but she'd have to think about it. She lied and told him she needed to make sure it didn't conflict with the book she was under contract to write. That she'd be in touch after speaking with her agent. Heath didn't seem annoyed or disappointed at all and had given information to her about the stepwell Manasa built to help her and her agent out. Riley had been so proud of her when Prem told her tale of deceit, swinging Prem around the kitchen Riley sung, 'You faked it till you made it!'

Prem had been proud of herself but also worried since then. If Heath found out her book deal was a lie, she'd have to figure out another lie in the future. She hoped it would all be worth it to see her name in print again.

6: When

After Prem looked into Manasa, Mirror Marsh, and the proposed dam which impacted flow to the Marigold River, she accepted Heath's offer and deadline. Heath gave her Manasa's contact info and they'd been in touch a lot, Manasa had been so friendly and warm towards Prem, calling to tell her exactly what she could expect when she showed up at Mirror Marsh for the interview, Prem relating to so much of what Manasa shared about her life before Mirror Marsh when she talked about the city nowadays.

Manasa had called again last night, right when Prem and Riley were snuggled on the couch watching a movie they had rented. Riley sighed in annoyance and again when Prem returned. It had been rude enough when Prem jumped up without even pausing the movie to answer the phone, ignoring her own rule about not answering the phone when it was a date night, but then Prem had talked on the phone for just a little too long. She couldn't help it though! Their conversation had flown so naturally, as though Manasa was an old friend.

Prem had felt so badly for treating Riley second to her job opportunity and had planned to make it up to Riley after she got home from the interview. Well, definitely after she had finished writing the first draft of her article. Prem would at least bring Riley dinner. She could grab takeout from that place that Riley liked, but they never went to because you had to eat at the bar. Prem was trying to feel positive about it all, everything would be okay with Riley and if Heath liked her story, maybe she'd get a regular gig. And who knows, maybe it wouldn't just be an interview, maybe Manasa and she would end up being good friends. Prem had a way of telling stories so readers truly saw her interview subject, even her most controversial subjects had to agree she was as objective as possible, telling all the truths she unearthed. Prem thought her writing was stronger than so many of The *Gazette*'s freelancers and then felt awful for even comparing herself to them. She didn't want to start dreaming about working at The *Gazette* before she'd even interviewed Manasa or written a single draft. But again, and again her mind kept returning to The *Gazette*, dreaming about a regular column, her photo displayed next to her name. Prem Morris in print.

This interview with Manasa was the exact reporting she had always wanted to do. When she first met Riley, that's what they had talked about when they laid together in bed, their feet intertwined, Prem curled up and looked at her fingers tracing scenes on Riley's belly. When she was young, a classmate had teased Prem, telling her that her skin was the color of a discarded acorn. She'd hated it for so long until she'd heard Riley describe her own skin to a friend as the color of a cat tail in a swamp. Their friend hadn't laughed at Riley's image, thinking Riley was putting herself down, but nodded and smiled, simply accepting Riley's descriptor. Prem hadn't decided when she would tell Riley that's what she was always tracing, Prem's spiky acorn rolling around Riley's cat tail, swaying in the swampy air. In so many big and little ways Riley had taught Prem how to love herself.

So, in those first few weeks, when they fell so fast for one another, they would share their dreams. When Riley could afford to, if her malpractice insurance allowed, if it didn't keep climbing in price, if she could find a medical space that would donate their clinic time, if it ever got safe to do house calls, if after if after if, she wanted to open a pay-what-you-can medical clinic. So that no one had to go without medical care. Prem would trace Riley's cat tail, swaying in the wind as she listened then began rolling her spiky, little acorn around Riley's lower belly as she told her how one day she'd have the funding to do deep field research, explaining how she wanted to show how convenient growing food could be, how important it was to report on the rise of community gardens and how they differed based on neighborhood. How even the biodiversity of pollinators differed based on how roads were laid and where you lived. For years Prem had been paging through the real estate sections of all the papers, watching the change in housing and real estate for decades and wanted to shine the light on landlords, neighborhood associations, and the barriers they were creating and not just for humans. Prem had so many plans, she just had to get this article written and in print first. And after that, maybe she would end up with an agent, a book deal. And after that, Prem would be rich, so she'd simply fund Riley's dream, her clinic for anyone who needed help.

7: Then

Ana happily sat at her new desk at her new job and sipped her chai from her stainless-steel bottle. Proud she was finishing up her first week at Willard's Wellness Waters and had impressed Mr. Paisley with her hard work and can-do attitude.

It had been a novel experience for Ana, she had spent her first day meeting his staff and cleaning up his executive suite. There had been some neglect in between Mr. Paisley's assistants, Ana had completely taken care of the weeks of newspapers that had piled up and had inventoried and tidied Mr. Paisley's personal kitchenette. There were only a few more hours until the weekend officially started, and Mr. Paisley had been in his office most of the day. Ana still couldn't figure out exactly what he did. Wayne, the blonde man with blue eyes Ana felt hard to resist when she interviewed for her new Executive's Assistant position had conspiratorially told her that Mr. Paisley was 'an ideas man' but Ana wasn't sure if Wayne had been joking and worse, she didn't know if she was the butt of the joke or if Mr. Paisley was. She liked every time Wayne stopped by her desk to say hi and wondered if he was friendly or flirtatious.

Mr. Paisley had told Ana that as long as she had completed her tasks for the day she could read, work on the crossword puzzle, complete her schoolwork, any quiet activity that wouldn't take her away from her desk and most importantly, her phone. She double checked the paper planner open in front of her and flipped to the next week. She had prepped everything she needed to for Monday's meetings and had tidied and organized everything she could find. Satisfied that her tasks were complete, she walked to the coffee table and snuck the local section out of that day's *Gazette*, and stepped back to her desk.

Initially she thought Mr. Paisley would judge her for reading instead of doing schoolwork but she thought back to their interview, which had gotten off to a rocky start, Ana uncomfortable about disclosing that her parents were Indian immigrants. She had learned most of the time it didn't matter that they were citizens, their brown skin made them outsiders, regardless. But Ana needed the job so practiced patience and after letting Mr. Paisley know her parents *had* moved from India, eventually found out that Mr. Paisley was a great admirer of India and Indians. Their customs and their culture. She shared that she had a plan to go back to school but wasn't quite ready yet, her parents' death had really been hard on her and she was struggling with the idea of being with her peers. Watching them party and study while she was grieving. She hadn't told Mr. Paisley all that of course, just let him know she wasn't a drop out, she wasn't a slacker, she would be returning to university one day.

And since Mr. Paisley knew she had every intention of returning to university one day, she didn't mind if he saw the newspaper on her desk. She would drop everything for him, as they had discussed in her interview. Ana took another sip of her chai, wishing it was warmer, and flipped through the local section, hoping for another update on Rufus. She was sad that there wasn't one, as there had been no updates at all on Rufus this week. She continued flipping through the pages and saw an update that upset her; the state's bounty had been so successful that citizens captured 374 snakes during the first week of the program. Ana grew angry when she read they were continuing to offer the bounty. If nearly 400 snakes were caught the first week, there may be no snakes left in a few years! She wanted to throw the paper when she read *This money could be yours, catch a Rock Rattlesnake today!*

Ana closed the paper, saddened that anyone would kill for money. She grew even more sad when she began wondering what she would do, if she hadn't gotten this amazing new job, if she refused to touch the money that was only in her bank because of her parents' tragic death, maybe she would grow so desperate to kill an innocent for a few cents too. Ana ran her fingernail over the fold of the newspaper, again and again, after she realized she would kill herself before she killed another, especially an innocent. She jumped when Wayne sat down on her desk, deep in thought she hadn't noticed anyone enter the Executive Suite.

"Turn that frown upside down, beautiful! It's Friday! I'm buying you a drink at Kilmer's."

8: When

Over the phone last night Manasa had confirmed no photography and Prem had had to call Heath after finishing the movie with Riley to tell him to cancel sending a staff photographer for the interview. Luckily, he had still been at his office. Manasa had promised to provide professional photos to the paper taken by Mirror Marsh photographers, who had captured some really great snapshots of the wildlife and beauty of the preserve.

Heath had sighed with annoyance just as Riley had and then snapped, "Ok, well go interview her tomorrow. What else are you going to do? Bring a spy camera? But make sure she understands we need *her* photo. Not just the marsh." Prem stood there long after he hung up, ashamed that he had just yelled at her like that. He didn't even know her, why would he treat her that way?

Having become somewhat familiar with the route to Manasa's Mirror Marsh and her new-to-her vehicle, Prem looked down at the tote bag next to her on the seat. Heath had given her a great idea and after she had dropped Riley off at the hospital, she had pulled into a strip mall and bought one of those brand-new disposable cameras. If it was just her and Manasa, she'd probably end up alone for just a little. The camera took twenty photos, which was more than she'd need. Prem knew her camera wasn't as nice as the ones the *Gazette* provided to their staff photographers, but she wasn't working with the *Gazette*'s budget. The ten dollars the disposable camera had cost wasn't even in Prem's budget.

The sun rising in the sky, the lies, the anger after letting Heath talk to her that way, the money problems, the drive, the nerves, every stressful feeling and uncertainty collided in Prem's brain and she found sweat dripping down the crevice between her breasts, tingling her face, causing her thighs to stick to the seats. The heat, the salt, the moisture all made the rashes on the back of her neck burn and Prem grew more uncomfortable knowing she wouldn't be taking her hands off the wheel or her eyes off the road until she stopped. Prem hated how the panic set again and again, one thing she stupidly tried to control; she knew she'd have nerves or be freaking out over something regardless of how well she planned, but it never ever made her problems any easier.

Prem didn't know what was wrong with her, her doctor had told her that if she didn't find an outlet, she was going to end up having a heart attack at a very young age.

You need to calm down and take better care of your body, these cortisol spikes are causing your rashes. I suggest starting with your sleep, I can write you a prescription, but don't scratch it, as tempting as it is. Just pat, you aren't molting, you aren't an animal, there's no need to scratch and injure yourself, get an infection, you just need some rest and to leave it alone. Can you try that? Just leave it alone and it will heal.

9: When

Prem looked forward to the billboards disappearing as she accelerated towards the peak of Hell's Hill. Paisley's Places Real Estate didn't just advertise the homes in the newly finished gated community for sale, they also advertised their own billboards, the advertising space on them at least. It made no sense to Prem; who drove out this way, anyway? Riley was right, it was creepy how they tried to get people to think, whether through billboards, ads in the paper, or the stories pitched to surround those ads. It was such a joke, Paisley's Places Real Estate didn't realize that anyone who found themselves out here likely couldn't afford one of those homes they were trying to sell.

Prem couldn't deny that it looked like a pretty magical place to live. Because it would take magic to afford the huge payment to live in your own little ecosystem, a guard stationed at all times to monitor access in, their own recreation and dining options (casual, upscale, or maybe just a stop at the café), spas and concierges, shared chefs and cooks, cleaning staff to help in your home, all vetted by Paisley's Places Real Estate's security clearances, which also allowed residents to safely walk or bike to a green space which held a farmer's market each weekend, all the goods and salespeople were safe, deemed acceptable to enter the gate, to sell their items and services for residential consumption.

Riley had gone on about the classism to Prem, who was well aware she was a have not who luckily was chosen for adoption by two halves who had. If things had been different, maybe she would be looking to move into luxury housing in the middle of not much else. A place where residents enjoyed their own private woods and walking trails, a manmade lake that had fish dumped in it regularly, hired beekeepers to help with the residents' gardens, all maintained by private groundskeepers, residents reaping what others had sowed and nourished for them. Riley had read about it in the *Gazette*, the club house with a pool heated all year long in case the pool in your own backyard or your neighbors' was not enough, the promise of community, if you could afford the cost, an opening of the knot, entrance to the cluster with their own private parties and holiday celebrations, fireworks, champagne, balloons, paid parivar. The gated community was so massive the advertisements bragged about the private transportation offered to get from place to place within the walls or to plan trips with others who self-selected this lifestyle outside the safety of the gate. Which was exactly why Prem wanted nothing to do with it; they could enjoy most of this in the city.

On the drive out Riley had laughed bitterly, acting as though she was deeply offended, playing the top of the hierarchy, insinuating, "Of course you'd convince yourself of that my dear, you won't ever be able to afford to live in Deer Commons!"

The billboards were such an eyesore to what was otherwise a very pleasant, scenic drive, if Prem hadn't been so afraid of driving that she could enjoy the views. Riley had gotten so angry at the sight of them, to her they hadn't just been an eyesore but a sign of everything wrong that was happening in their generation.

"This shit is SO fucked, Prem! They're advertising creating their own little nation, their own class of citizens. Deer Commons? There is nothing common about the people who live there or in that place! A place for those that can afford to live there and those who work there in exchange for room, board, and a little bit of spending money," Riley jeered after they passed the billboard advertising remaining available jobs in Deer Commons, gardeners, nursing assistants, medics, housekeepers, and the scariest job category, monitoring assistants, which offered a sign-on bonus for those who had prior experience in security or surveillance. *Call to apply today!*

Prem had agreed with Riley and let her go on her tirade. She wondered if Riley ever got so upset over the other billboards, the ones that reminded Prem of her own origin story. Her mother had always told Prem it was the most loving thing to do, and Prem understood that was true. The pain of that truth hit her almost every day. To Prem the worst billboards on the drive to Mirror Marsh were the anti-abortion billboards, the advertisements Paisley's Places Real Estate made money off of that were lies. Advertisements that gave false expectations and false information. Prem had been fired from the *Only Daily* over her coverage of one of these organizations, just recently discovering her pride over being fired thanks to Riley convincing her she *had* done the right thing. Prem's article had exposed their truth, though they promised health examinations and STD tests, saying you could get free medical care if you were pregnant and *just* came to them, their intent was to convince you to keep the pregnancy, to not provide birth control, to stay in a situation that you had wanted to get out of when you came to them for help. *Children are such a gift, we're here for you. No one's really ever ready to be a mom.*

Prem would never be able to understand, what kind of person would lie to someone who asked for help?

10: Now

Elongating each side of her torso, Jani noticed the sides of her ribs, the spaces between them broadening and enjoying the sensation of her intercostal muscles, which she rarely noticed. Jani reached beyond the curling branches for the sky, wanting to feel deeper and deeper into her chest, back, and sides, she wanted to notice all that she never got to notice. Jani kept pushing her feet away, into Mother Earth, hoping she would take no disrespect from this practice. After all, Jani was just playing at being a tree. Vrkasana. Jani thought of all the similarities between her and the oak she balanced under. Mother Earth was their home and provided for them both.

Jani took a deep inhale and then drew her arms back to her sides slowly as she exhaled. Branches returning to their trunk, a difference between her and this magnificent tree. She stood in stillness for another few breaths, listening to the birds sing to one another about her presence and catching the buzz the many insects made. She smiled, knowing the cinnamon they grew actually helped a little; the buzzing of bugs was never this loud back home.

Jani walked a few steps away from the majestic oak she had taken her seated break with, grateful for the oak's ample protection from Surya and for the strength of the tree trunk allowing her to lean on it. Knowing she didn't have to be so strong was possible when no one was watching. Because she had lived inside and out of Deer Commons, The Council had higher expectations of her. She had fought to keep a solemn face when they told her their strange enemies could climb walls. How even touching their skin could result in death. Jani hadn't known what to do but nod in understanding. She had been so young and Momma had always been worried Jani wouldn't know science, so Jani had pretended she had. That her momma had taught her that same thing, even though she hadn't. Momma had told Jani, "If you leave them alone, they'll likely leave you alone, darling. You don't gotta do nothing but nothing."

They had liked Jani's answers. Jani liked when they liked her answers. That was then and today Jani liked that The Council liked her. Relied on her. That she was important to Deer Commons. That maybe she could build a life there with Hans.

She didn't know for sure though. Hans had never brought it up and no one else in Deer Commons was in a permanent relationship outside of their citizenship class. If Hans felt the same as Jani, *he* would have to ask.

Those who weren't full citizens of Deer Commons didn't have access to the Scriptorium and relied on The Council to interpret their law.

Drishti had full citizenship and apprenticed in the Scriptorium. Not for the first time, Jani regretted her reliance on The Council for the pleasant life she led.

11: When

Prem kept her eyes on the road and her breath intentional to avoid slipping further into panic. Each time the truck went over a bump she anticipated flying out of her seat. She thought of her mother, who had always reacted with protection in those types of moments, a drive where she had been bouncing around, her mother would have told her to hang on to her seat or if a sudden stop occurred, her mother's arm would shoot out in front of Prem's torso, a weak insurance in case Prem's physical seatbelt failed.

"Can you believe these idiots?" Prem remembered her dad's complaint, "They're trying to make a law forcing us to wear seat belts. It should be my choice!"

Prem had sensed not wearing a seat belt would make him proud so never did with him, just like she sensed he was the type of man who would donate money to those fake medical centers Paisley's Places Real Estate advertised.

Prem hadn't visited her parents in a few years, but the last time she had, her mom had returned to that protective behavior. A drive to the supermarket turned into whiplash for Prem's mom. She had still stuck her hand out, trying to protect Prem as she had for so many years of her youth. Prem hadn't anticipated she would have that same instinct.

When they had returned home, without groceries, Prem's dad hadn't even noticed. It was only after he saw Prem massaging her mother's neck that he realized something had happened. When Prem's mother assured him she was fine, she let it slip that it was a good thing everyone had been wearing their seat belts.

"You can't save anyone's life with a little of cloth, it remains God's plan," he preached, shaking his head as he walked away, "My body, my choice, except when it comes to these damn seat belts."

12: When

Prem's mother always seemed to be almost apologetic for Prem's dad's misogynistic behaviours. That same night her dad had dismissed seat belts being helpful he had grumbled about being hungry. Prem had snapped at him, telling him that the fridge was where it had always been and Prem's mom's shoulders hunched, releasing Prem from her massage duties. Their daughter objected, shouted that she'd make dinner, and Prem's dad sat on the couch while the two Morris women reheated leftovers. Prem's mom kept up cleaning as Prem fumed, clanging dishes and utensils, wishing it was possible to infuriate her dad.

It maddened Prem how her mother was always an example of patience. She was grateful for her, for despite all that she had lived through, with Prem she had always been very vocal of her opinion that *all* women had the right to abortion and reproductive health care. In elementary school her mom had conspired with other moms to get together, to teach their children about menstruation and what living with a period actually was like, to share tips for handling bathrooms and leaving the house. Only Sally's mom took her up on her offer and Prem knew it was because Sally had not one friend.

So, on a night that Prem's dad had bowling league, Prem and Sally learned about their reproductive organs as Prem's mom poured dosa batter onto their hotplate, starting with the uterus and cervix, plopping down two ovaries, and then dripping out the fallopian tubes to connect them.

"It's not accurate, but it's close!" Prem's mom had joked to Sally's mom.

"Okay," Sally's mom replied as she sat at the kitchen table with her ankles crossed, far from the hot plate.

Sally's mom hadn't even bothered with the usual niceties, the offer to be in touch, to host next time. She just thanked Prem's mom for an interesting dinner and then pulled Sally out of their house.

Prem's mom returned to the kitchen to clean up, and Prem worried about whether she'd have fewer friends than Sally the next day.

13: Then

"Alright, well now you know Willard and I are brothers. It's so cute you thought it was a coincidence we shared the last name," Wayne laughed, his smile made Ana's heart skip a beat, "I told you about my name, you tell me about yours Ahhhh-naaa."

Ana laughed nervously, unsure if Wayne was poking fun at her, flirting, or had some other nefarious reason for asking. This was only her second time at a bar and her first time drinking on a date. Ana cringed internally as she realized Wayne never said this was a date, he must've invited her here as a joke, or maybe just to be friendly. He was her boss's brother!

"Oh, it's a boring story. I'd much rather hear about how long you've worked for Willard's Wellness Waters," Ana hoped her smile made Wayne feel a tenth of the way his had just made her feel.

"Well, since Pa gave Willard the money and told him he had to hire me once I graduated. He paid for school, so I owed him," Wayne revealed bitterly.

"Not your dream job?" Ana asked.

"Nope. My dream job is living off my interest earned."

"Your interest?"

"Yeah, I want to go into real estate, investment properties, rental units, all of it, but Pa said I was too young."

"Oh, I'm sorry. That sounds like it might be a lot more work though. I rent and I don't know how to fix anything; I'm so glad my landlord is willing to help, but I couldn't imagine having to run to a rental property in the middle of the night to fix something."

Wayne scoffed, "I'd pay someone for that."

"Oh."

"I mean, everyone invests differently," Wayne corrected gently, trying to adjust his harsh reaction to Ana's positivity.

"What do you think it would take for you to get into real estate?"

"Pa said I could support Willard's business while saving up to start my own. It was clear to us both he wasn't paying for everyone's dreams. And Willard's the oldest, so he got the chance to start a business before me. He knows. He said he'll pay me back for helping him."

"I hope it doesn't take you too long to save up," Ana bubbled hopefully.

"I'm waiting and saving. That's all I can do," Wayne called the bartender over with a curl of his index finger. Ana picked up her drink and thought of what she could say that might impress Wayne while the bartender mixed their drinks. She knew she shouldn't talk about herself too much if she wanted to keep his interest, but also knew that if she was quiet for too much longer, he may lose interest.

"What about you," Wayne slid her drink over, "Willard said you were taking a break from University?"

"Yeah, something happened with my parents, and I had to step back. But I'm not dropping out!" Ana insisted.

"No, of course not, you're too sexy to miss out on undergrad."

"Heh, thanks," Ana blushed. She swallowed the last of her first drink, holding back a shudder before placing her hand around the second drink Wayne ordered for her.

"Ana, tell me more, what's up with your parents? I bet they're dicks like mine. My dad threatened to stop paying for my degree if I didn't get better grades. Party too hard? It doesn't look like it was the Freshman Fifteen. Why work instead of going to school?" Wayne encouraged Ana to open up, reaching his hand towards hers on the bar.

Ana released her grip on her cocktail and snaked her fingers towards Wayne's in return, "I don't enjoy talking about myself too much. It's probably boring for you, right?"

Wayne stood and scooted his stool closer towards Ana's, "I don't think that could ever be. Since we met last week, all I have been able to think about is how I *must* know you."

Ana felt herself getting hot and thought of taking a sip of her vodka soda. As she looked up at Wayne, she hoped he'd sit down but instead he coiled his fingers together with hers and leaned down to whisper in her ear.

"Wayne! Sit!" Ana laughed at his flirtation.

"What? I said what I said," Wayne admitted with mock guilt before sitting back down.

"How about you walk me home before we try what you suggested?" Ana felt her confidence growing with her second drink, empowered that Wayne found her so beautiful and interesting.

"I can't wait to walk you home every night," Wayne said as he snaked his hand from Ana's grip to under her skirt.

Ana pulsed from the excitement; she had never felt a man's hand so high on her thigh before.

14: When

It had been so natural for Prem to expose the hypocrisy of the org when she had gone undercover, it always shocked Riley when she learned of one of Prem's white lies but hadn't batted an eye when she learned how Prem had gotten her story. She had simply walked right in their doors, pretending she was worried she was pregnant, meekly explaining she had missed her period, was hoping it was just late but unable to afford one of those at home pregnancy tests with the impossible to follow instructions.

Prem had taken the necessary science to graduate from university but missed period or not, no one had the desire to pretend to be a scientist, hiding the tubes and solutions, a secret chemist for two hours waiting to find a result that held a seventy percent accuracy, meaning making sure you bought two tests and taking another one, wasting two more hours. From their talks on the phone, Prem knew Manasa believed water was our most precious resource, but Prem wondered if Manasa had ever considered it was what Prem thought was most precious, time.

Sure, going to the doctor was an option for those who could afford it, knew how to schedule an appointment, could find transportation on their own but how many people would find out, who would be in the waiting room, who on the staff would gossip, what if a bill or follow-up reminder was sent to the mailing address they made you provide. The simple solution just wasn't always safe, not everyone felt a missed period was good news, a blessing. So, Prem went undercover and learned how this org operated, sitting in their office for an entire afternoon, in a strip mall not too different from the one where she picked up her disposable camera. In the end, they had no medical test but used what anyone could purchase at the local supermarket. Two hours spent waiting for the results and another two hours praying with them for guidance.

While she waited for her negative result, the staff that claimed to be pro-life sought to comfort Prem, telling her not to worry, how they would help her if she was pregnant, she had nothing to worry about, the baby would be cared for, an abundance headed for her and her little one, *if* she attended bible study or their parenting classes or volunteered in their daycare then she would be rewarded with *Coins for Mommies*, large metal discs with their logo imprinted on them, which she could exchange for anything she needed, diapers, food, blankets, whatever was in their storeroom that had been donated by those who no longer needed them.

Their system had been explained to her as they thumbed through medical illustrations of babies in utero, letting Prem know the importance of her decision, working to convince her again and again of the multiple sins she would be committing if she tried to leave their doors. They finally allowed her to leave when Prem asked them of their degrees and their licenses, asking them why exactly it was that they wore white lab coats although they had no medical expertise, just donated medical equipment. Prem had wondered how many bellies their shared donated stethoscope had touched, hands without gloves or their best intentions tenderly touching their bellies.

The most surprising thing from Prem's investigation was that before she departed she had expected them to throw condoms at her, naively thinking they would try to convince her with information on hormonal or barrier birth control but all there had been was a poster in their sad waiting room, a diagram loosely explaining the ineffective rhythm method.

Prem had felt high when she had stacked her pages, thinking she had written it, the one piece that would make her stand out, had submitted the best article she had ever written to Eric, her editor at the *Only Daily*, and had been let go before the end of the week. Given a small box for her things and an escort to her car in the parking garage, Prem thanking Cam, her friend in security, for carrying the light box for her. Cam showed he was embarrassed that this was part of his job, apologizing with a smile.

Later, Eric had invited her for coffee to explain what had happened and why he couldn't be a reference for her. An investor in the paper was running a political campaign under the guise of family values, Eric couldn't be seen as going up against him. Eric agreed with everything in Prem's piece and looked truly upset that it would never make it to publication. Unfortunately, Eric wasn't so upset that he would be a future reference for Prem, he needed his job and Prem's name had been noticed and marked, it was unlikely anyone would hire her.

"Maybe you could look into teaching ESL?" Eric had suggested, "I could definitely be a reference for something like that, but if it came back that I recommended you to another paper, I'd be toast. You should stay quiet on the abortion shit, it's unpleasant anyway, maybe switch gears and try with a smaller paper after you take a break."

Prem smiled and nodded as she sipped her coffee; Eric's treat, of course. She understood and agreed with him and told Eric so when he told her he had to run, apologizing and promising they'd get together soon.

Prem *had* understood why Eric said nothing, didn't print the article anyway. He had his own career to think about and after all, who was Prem to him? When she had called Eric to confirm she could list him as a reference on the jobs she was applying for outside of the publishing world, he never once picked up the phone or returned the messages she left with his assistant.

Eric just kind of agreed, Prem had realized. He didn't agree enough to inconvenience his own ambition.

15: When

Prem couldn't wait to be done driving, realizing she was spiraling and told herself to find a distraction to calm down, searching her brain for a visualization. Ever since her physician had made that 'joke' about molting Prem couldn't stop thinking of snakes, her patches of skin that were flaking off in scales doing exactly what her doctor had described, if she wanted, she could probably peel layers off and leave them behind, traces of her existence. She had thought of making that joke to Riley but didn't want Riley to know how bad it really was, to hear Riley say she was worried about Prem, that Prem was sounding like one of her patients.

Prem took a breath, and then another, reminding herself that before she finally went to the doctor, after obsessing over her dry skin, she had convinced herself she had skin cancer, that a growth that invaded the body's largest organ; but that hadn't been true. Prem was really, fantastic at making little problems big ones in her head. She was just stressed because today was a monumental day for her. She didn't need to self-sabotage.

Prem thought of her doctor's *other* recommendations and how her new therapist would suggest making her snakeskin worries into a calming meditation. *Think about it this way, what's the worst thing that would happen if you really turned into a snake?*

The answer was so easy, that Riley would see her like that. She wanted Riley to be happy, not be with someone who freaked out over every little thing, whose dry scaly skin meant she was becoming a reptile.

Prem took another breath, rationalizing that it was natural she was thinking of snakes, Manasa had explained it was likely they'd see a few when they took their tour.

"Rock rattlesnakes like to sun on the stone, but we will just steer away when we see them, that's what I do so I'm not asking you to do something I wouldn't do," Manasa had warned, "They don't want to hurt us so please remember we are actually in *their* home and respect that."

Prem had thanked Manasa when she agreed. She had liked that about Manasa, in just a few conversations she had been so clear to Prem about where to go, what to expect, and what to do.

16: Now

Jani worried about her crew, the Guardians remaining had to be close to breaking down, it could only be expected after witnessing everything they had. Every horror. Those who had only ever lived within Deer Commons had never had to get used to it. Their walls had kept them safe. They'd always been so lucky. Even before the collapse everything had been so safe for them.

Jani fussed with her pack as she thought of the villagers she was told to protect. They had never seen anything like it, a coordinated attack. There had been signs, they had all been told of tales of plagues and pestilence. Stories recorded in the scriptorium, told in the nurseries.

Jani watched two melanistic squirrels dance across a branch of the oak and she remembered one of Momma's tales, the story of a village who banished Saaya and all their friends, a fear of black cats causing rodent populations to multiply and run the citizens out of their very own villages. Homes abandoned from a plague carried by the furry rodents who overpopulated nearly instantly. Momma said that the fairy tale was based on a real-life story. Jani didn't want to abandon Deer Commons like those pathetic villagers in Momma's story had done. Even as a young girl Jani had asked why they didn't just welcome Saaya and all cats back.

"When creatures who help are kept out, why would they return to help again?" Momma had replied.

17: When

Prem could only relax for a moment before she scared herself, something that happened much too often when she tried to relax. For her birthday Riley had treated Prem to a pedicure and Prem just couldn't enjoy it, worried about how much the workers were being paid and whether the tools were sanitized, if the tub she soaked her feet in had been cleaned properly. She had spent the whole time waiting for it to be over instead of relaxing, which was what Riley had instructed.

Despite her intentional breathwork, Prem was panicking, feeling like an imposter, doubting what Riley meant with the constant advice to fake it. She flipped her gaze from the road to the steering wheel and saw the lines on her knuckles as she gripped it, disgusted by the dry skin on the back of her hands, grey and slightly painful as it stretched to meet Prem's need for control of the steering wheel, irritated as she had massaged the salve in less than an hour ago.

Prem grew angry realizing how tense her body was, thinking of how it couldn't relax for more than a few moments before her brain caused her muscles to become all coiled up like a snake.

Prem returned to her pretend play, a professional driver would keep their eyes on the road and so she kept her eyes ahead of her, not letting her fear of the steep climb in Riley's truck seep into her worries anymore. One worry at a time Prem told herself, one problem at a time, imagining how she could relax the coil with her breath, but not able to relax for even a full breath cycle before tensing again, gaze penetrating through the windshield to force focus on the dirt road as she strained against her deep breath she imagined a snake from Mirror Marsh sneaking into the cab, coiling around her ribs, slowly suffocating her, crushing all of the air out of her lungs, her diaphragm not being able to move up or down, no expansion, only collapse.

Prem jerked the steering wheel, sharply veering over to the side of the road, the truck uneven as it dealt with the steep climb towards the peak of Hell's Hill. Prem steadied herself, letting out a sound of air, feeling the sting of it on the back of her hands where the scaly skin was raw, as she corrected the steering wheel back towards the dirt path leading to Mirror Marsh. She had almost driven herself off of fucking Hell's Hill, worried about a snake. Making up yet another scenario to freak out about.

"What the fuck is wrong with you?" Prem questioned herself out loud. Soon she'd have to drive the pickup down the steep peak of Hell's Hill and needed to be focused, in charge of her mind and her body so she didn't lose control again, tumble to her death. Prem rarely drove, and this was only her second time driving down a dirt road, reminding her again of how lucky she was to live somewhere with public transit and paved roads, it must've been so hard traveling in the days of horse-drawn carriages or for those in the world who have to walk everywhere on dirt paths or create their own.

"Get it together Prem," she spoke aloud to herself once again, "This story won't be about a lone reporter who died driving off Hell's Hill."

This was the opportunity of a lifetime for Prem, a second chance, an invitation back into the industry she had almost given up on after being blacklisted after making the wrong people upset. Prem wondered if the investors who took her career away thought about her as much as she thought of them.

Prem released her foot from the gas, slowing down as she neared the peak of Hell's Hill. Her heart in her throat as she thought of how she knew those investors didn't give a shit.

18: When

Prem found the descent down Hell's Hill more intimidating than the drive up. If it wasn't for her seatbelt, she could imagine so easily floating off of her seat, hitting her head or going through the windshield. Prem *almost* laughed out loud at her ability to think of the worst potential outcomes.

Prem would be at the stepwell soon enough and began giving herself a pep talk, Heath selected *her* for this piece.

It didn't show up when she played board games or sports but with school or work, Prem had always been this way. Always looking for a way to be the best, the top of her class, the star reporter, the sought after employee.

Prem slowly coasted down Hell's Hill as she thought about how she'd always had a problem with this. Making friends had always been hard, she had a few people she spoke to, but Riley was probably the only person who really knew her. Her mom thought she knew Prem but she really only knew what she expected of her daughter, not what was going on inside her daughter's head or her heart.

She often wondered about her mother, her real mother that is, her biological mother who no one knew. When Prem had turned 18 her mom had given her the contact information for the adoption agency but it had been long defunct. Prem tried so hard to not hold resentment, but why had it taken so long for her mom to give her that number?

Prem wondered why her mind always moved to sabotage her, she could have thought of Riley's hug from the morning, the fact that she had Amelia's friendship, that Heath had awarded *her* with his big Earth Day piece but her mind always pushed her to thoughts of death. Her urge to self-sabotage was something her therapist had pointed out to her when Prem explained she was *only* there because her doctor recommended it. Piece by piece her therapist put the puzzle together, learning the actual reason, not even bothering to scribble in her notepad as she listened to Prem speak on the rashes that were popping up; rough, dry, red, scaly patches that Prem thought about constantly, worried about going places in case she couldn't bring or apply her salves, this change in her skin hadn't happened before, but was coming back again and again and again. It had to mean something but as Prem explained, her doctor said it most likely attributed to stress.

And what is it about your life that is causing you stress?

19: Then

Ana was straightening the newspapers and arranging the magazines in the reception area of Mr. Paisley's executive suite before his first meeting of the day. She looked up at the clock and saw there was about twenty minutes before she would get the coffee ready for them. As Ana was returning to her desk Mr. Paisley stepped out of his office to request she join him for a few minutes.

Ana entered his office and sat in the same chair she had for her interview, just a few weeks back. She watched as Mr. Paisley paced the room and wondered what she had done to get in trouble. If it had anything to do with Wayne.

Ana fidgeted and cleared her throat as Mr. Paisley returned to his desk. She wanted to ask if everything was okay but was worried that would make him even more upset than he already was.

"Ana, I wanted to take a few minutes this morning to say how pleased I am with your initiative around the office. You know the last few girls always *asked* what they had to do but you just go ahead and do it!"

Ana felt a whoosh of relief surge through her body, she had done nothing wrong, and she would not be fired.

"Thank you, Mr. Paisley, I really have enjoyed my first few weeks here," Ana shared with a small smile.

"Ana, I know I've trained you that the Executive Suite restrooms and kitchenette are for my use only but I have been so impressed with your care for me and our space that I want you to know you can use the Ladies' Executive Restroom."

"Oh, wow. Thank you, Mr. Paisley," Ana voiced sincerely. Mr. Paisley only had three rules, and he had made them clear on Ana's first day. First, she was to always address him as 'Mr. Paisley', *yes even if my father shows up to WWW you'll address me as such*. It had been hard for Ana at first, Willard wasn't that much older than her, but she understood his need for respect. Mr. Paisley's second rule was that Ana was always at her desk before or after his meetings. He had explained he wanted her there to take down notes or escort his guests out of the building so that he didn't have to. The ultimate rule was that no employees were to use the Executive Suite's Restrooms or Kitchenette. They were for his personal use only. Ana was allowed to use the Kitchenette if she needed to prepare him a snack or offer guests a beverage but if she wanted a place to eat, she would have to head down to the Staff Breakroom, which was a total disaster. She had seen it on her first day and thanked Ganesh that she lived close enough to walk home and back for her lunch every day.

Ana had laughed to herself when Mr. Paisley had told her she had to walk downstairs to use the bathroom or to eat a snack. It was so silly that he had all these spaces to himself and the silliest was that no one was using the women's restroom in the Executive Suite. Mr. Paisley's rules forced Ana to run up and down the stairs several times to make sure she made it back before some of Mr. Paisley's back-to-back meetings, which made it less of a joke to her. And so, she was truly grateful that he offered this small kindness to her. Ana knew he didn't *have* to grant her permission to use his private bathroom.

"No, thank you Ana," Mr. Paisley stood and walked out from around his desk. Ana followed his cue and stood as well, assuming he was escorting her to his door but Mr. Paisley stopped and stared at her. Ana stood still, unsure of what to do. Mr. Paisley had frozen for just a moment, however. It seemed he woke back up and smiled at Ana, gesturing for her to walk towards the door to her world, the reception suite.

As Ana walked towards the door, she felt Mr. Paisley's hand on the small of her back. She told herself he was just being polite, even when he stood with his hand on the door handle, Ana recognizing she could not leave without his approval.

Mr. Paisley and Ana stood at the door and smiled at one another.

"Well, I better get that coffee on!" Ana exclaimed, knowing she had plenty of time before Mr. Paisley's nine am.

Mr. Paisley shook his head and smiled, "That is exactly what I'm talking about Ana! Thank you again for your hard work and for being you. I have never seen Wayne so happy. At work or at home. You keep making him happy."

Mr. Paisley turned the handle on the door and opened it, lightly tapping Ana on the ass to let her know it was time to get back to work and brew some coffee.

20: When

She had done her research on the very strange location of Mirror Marsh and Manasa Moody, patron of her very own public waterspace. Manasa had led an incredibly ordinary life up until the tragic death of her parents as far as Prem's research could determine. At a very young age she decided to purchase this swampy land. At that age Prem had still been hungover most mornings and Manasa had spent those years learning about finance and property law, engineering, and permits. Formally naming it Mirror Marsh, building a replica stepwell, and then opening it up to the public. Manasa had no worries about lawsuits or maintenance from Prem's research, and she planned to ask Manasa more about that. She took her eyes off the road to check the time on the clock in the cab.

Prem leaned forward in the cab as she thought about how there was no parking lot where she was headed, visitors were expected to pull over to mowed areas on the side of the road, Manasa had insisted on no pavement, no parking lots. This had surprised Prem and Manasa had admitted she wanted to welcome all to visit but had never wanted to create a car friendly experience, hence no formal ribbon cutting, just a simple announcement in the paper.

She understood as Manasa had explained, the addition of the stepwell had been a big change to the ecosystem as it was, adding all the extra cement needed for a parking lot would change the watershed significantly. Prem had listened in awe as Manasa told her the fewer visitors at one time the better, Mirror Marsh wasn't set up to handle the waste that came from humans picnicking or cleaning their cars before they headed back home. Manasa was so clear in her intent, Prem wished she could be like that one day, she thought after she hung the phone back on its receiver. She stood there in admiration, understanding completely Manasa's dedication to environmentalism. She hoped she could tell Manasa how excited she was to learn from her, how much Manasa offered to teach the readers of the *Gazette*. Prem wanted to be Manasa's friend and at the same time was desperate to prove herself and look like a professional.

21: When

Prem slowed down even more as the road flattened, tensing and groaning at every bump on the path she wouldn't describe as a road, rolling on the Earth, her lower back and right hip becoming more and more uncomfortable at how she chose to sit behind the wheel, leaning forward, shoulders pulled up to her ears, trying to anticipate everything she couldn't see. She reminded herself about what Riley had said when she had complained on their practice drive out to Mirror Marsh, that if Prem only focused on the path directly in front of her, she would miss everything else on this drive to Mirror Marsh. After that she leaned back into her seat slightly and could take in how beautiful the site Manasa had chosen was. The view overtook her, Prem's eyes filled with saltwater and when she reached out for Riley, she found Riley had been reaching out for her too. As they traveled upon Hell's Hill they felt the real-world slip away, fingers moving like the waves they saw in the meadows, a primordial rhythm, cat tails and acorns not in view and still part of the dance.

Without Riley beside her Prem thought about how cat tails turned to fluff, dispersing with the wind. And how some acorns relied on fire to be freed.

22: Now

Jani had been debating a plague of fur versus a plague of scales and had decided that a plague of furry creatures with tiny teeth would be much more tolerable than the plague of scales and fangs Deer Commons had been cursed with.

They had always been safe from the serpents. Why now?

Surya was feeling strong today, Jani could feel warmth even on the winds which touched her skin. She walked through Mirror Marsh and thought of how ancient this land was. She had witnessed it on her break with the acorns, after the long journey up and down Hell's Hill. The ancient oak tree must have witnessed much, Jani saw the tree's life, the growth of strong stable roots, woody, and snaking above the ground as they stretched out twistedly from the oak's enormous trunk. Jani considered the roots underground as well, wondering if the oak had warned the rest of Mirror Marsh of her presence. Momma had taught her that some plants could communicate underground. If things had been different, Jani born within Deer Commons, she could go to the Scriptorium, ask if anyone knew. But if she had been born in Deer Commons, she wouldn't be out here, wondering.

Jani pondered how much the oak knew about her, what warning it had sent out to the plants she'd meet on her way. She had doubted at first, pretended to believe alongside her neighbors but they had mentioned the oak in the legend, it was still healthy and strong. Everything here was. Jani understood her neighbors concern now that she saw parts of the Legend of Eadwayne were true.

23: When

With no convenient parking lot available Prem had a decision to make, finding the best spot to pull over. She wanted to walk for a bit to describe to the *Gazette*'s readers what it was like to be within the marsh and discover the stepwell. She also didn't want to have to walk back to her car in the dark.

24: When

Prem was impressed when Manasa explained she didn't feel it was right to take credit for the construction of the stepwell, that she only felt comfortable taking credit for payment.

"I'll bring the business card for the civil engineering firm I contracted with, I had the vision, but they were the ones who are the actual experts on creating a sustainable monument," Manasa chatted as Prem leaned against the kitchen wall, mindlessly running a cloth along the counter, "They'll be able to give an expert opinion on the impact a parking lot would have on the water table too. You'll be in direct contact with the best experts in our state on hydrology and environmental landscapes."

Prem glanced at the clock again, wondering what time she'd get home to Riley. This had been such a long drive and once again she wondered about Manasa's desire to spend so much time and energy building something that was so hard to get to. Exactly who would visit a place beyond dirt roads with no parking lots? Did she want visitors at all? Questions she'd ask Manasa soon enough.

25: Now

Jani began stepping with less force, traveling with a lighter step. The ground was so muddy here, she had to be careful, she was blindly walking forward in the grass.

Finding a flat patch of earth Jani stood still, listening to the wind rustling, noticing the difference in the orchestra's song here in the meadow and its similarities to the song which played through the oak's obovate leaves.

Evaluating the weight of the earth underneath her boots, Jani began swaying. First from her toes to her heels, easing the weight of her body forward and back while she leaned on the earth. This always reminded her of Momma, *this was how the collapse happened darling, humanity had lost our physical connection to Mother Earth and it no longer felt a part of us, so we hurt it as we sometimes hurt that which we don't know, can't figure out how to understand.*

Jani had fought to keep that connection, after learning that from Momma, the smallest bit of information shared from the only blood she knew from the before times. Hans would catch her sometimes, tickling her fingers across growing plants as they walked sometimes, or wiggling her fingers into the dirt in the gardens. Deer Commons could be so sterile with all of its rules and protocols to maintain their ways of living and to keep disease and violence far away. Of course, he would find it strange at first that his neighbor would bend down to feel the fuzzy softness of the lamb's ear growing in a neighbor's kitchen garden when they were supposed to be on patrol.

How strong Mother Earth was to support her, us, them. Jani found equal weight in both feet, gently softening her knees in order to find stillness under the farthest reaches of the wind's song. Her mind kept wandering back, wondering if they were keeping safe and if the remaining working Guardians were listening to Hans or showing up for their shifts. Jani prayed nothing had happened to Hans.

26: When

Prem adjusted her cotton tote bag on her shoulder as she examined the newest path ahead. It showed signs of travel she wasn't used to, patterns fossilized from the once muddy road. They had been, big, wide tires; the road had certainly been traveled upon but there wasn't any sign of such travel today.

Prem's mind crawled, it was odd that Manasa had changed her mind about the feature. At first she wanted no publicity and then she called Heath to invite state and possibly national coverage?

"Strange, right?" Prem questioned Riley.

Riley told her to stop being so paranoid, "You gotta stop being so suspicious babe. A bad thing isn't always coming. You don't always gotta look out."

In the viper's pit which was Prem's stomach, something was telling her things with Manasa or in Mirror Marsh wouldn't be what they seemed. They just couldn't be. There had been no buzz about it, Manasa's public water utility project that Prem could find with no public or business sponsorships. It was like Manasa had lived on dal chawal, lived a yogini's life in order to spend every cent rehabilitating Mirror Marsh and building this stepwell.

Prem reminded herself that the comfort calling her was from self-sabotage, that she needed to stay calm, that there was no need to scare herself before her interview. That even if Manasa had lived the life of an ascetic, she wouldn't be the first to have done so. Riley was right, she didn't need always feel nervous, she didn't need to be suspicious. She could let people be. Not make up stories about them.

As she walked off the dried mud, onto the mowed path through the prairie, she was in awe of the landscape surrounding her, it seemed there was no end to the prairie and oak savanna landscape when you were in the middle of it, surrounded in every direction. She put her arms out and slowly swirled in a circle, her fingertips tickled by the grass, her ears deafened by the sound of the wind, the songbirds, a croak here, a squawk there.

Prem's hand patted her tote bag, her thoughts descending into dread again. She was alone with not much civilization nearby. A notepad, a few pens, her tape recorder, her wallet, keys, and a disposable camera were the protection Prem had in this incredibly isolated spot.

27: When

Prem wandered along the mowed path, snaking between the tall grasses, looking out for little critters and their dens, taking notes on the lives of Mirror Marsh. She distracted herself from her thoughts, Riley knew where she was but Riley would be busy at work, they never talked to one another during the day unless Riley called Prem on lunch, but even that was usually scheduled. They had planned to catch up at their apartment, Riley relying on public transit to get back just in case Prem was deep in her draft. She had explained to Riley her process, how she wanted to get the story down as soon as she got home. It was so nice of Riley to offer to be inconvenienced and Prem fought until Riley insisted.

"Prem, it would make *me* happy if you just took my truck," Riley had said, both throwing their hands in the air out of annoyance and then laughing at how silly they were. Prem had been so relieved at the simple solution to how she would get to Mirror Marsh and back to the city. Heath had dangled her name as the byline on the front page of the Sunday local section and Prem jumped and asked how high after she was in the air, agreeing to drive to the middle of nowhere when she didn't even have a car.

A similarity Prem had found she had with Manasa. No record of any vehicle or driver's licensure. What were the chances that both women had made it to her mid-thirties without buying a car?

Heath had mentioned it once when he checked in, "No pressure Prem but I'm pretty sure this lady thinks she's like a real deal eco-warrior. No credit, no car, no gas, childless, has always lived so frugally. Our subscribers are going to go nuts learning that someone lives this way. Nothing's more controversial than making someone feel bad about their choices, urging them to do better."

Amelia and her roommate must not have told Heath too much about Prem.

Prem thought it was odd Heath didn't describe Manasa as boring, that was what she usually got when people found out she wasn't a mother. Because she had acquired wealth, Manasa's choices were exotic not timid like Prem's.

From Heath's description Manasa sounded a little mentally off, never buying a new outfit, wearing shoes and socks until they could no longer be repaired or mended and even then just wearing them for as long as it became detrimental. Not everyone had time to sit around and darn socks. And in fact, Prem truly believed time was the world's most precious resource, that Manasa used it to sit in the middle of Mirror Marsh, extracted from society, just further confirmed Prem's belief that it was acceptable to be eccentric if you had saved up enough to contribute to the betterment of all.

She was just slightly younger than Manasa, yet Manasa had dedicated her entire adult life to building this stone waterspace, in the middle of a hard to get to place, while Prem was still figuring out how to buy groceries and pay rent. How was it that Prem, with so many privileges struggled so damn much and Manasa who had comparably less fortune was so easily able to glide towards her goal?

28: Now

Jani walked, disappointed with how much she had lost. How quickly she had forgotten about the variety of trees and all the other plants she had relied on and lived with for the years she had walked the Borderlands with Momma. The safety and structure within the walls of Deer Commons had partially erased her memories of all the wild growth outside of them. Momma called anywhere without rule the Borderlands, all those open spaces where they didn't know who to be. On her way to Hell's Hill, Jani couldn't be certain whether she was being watched but right here, in the open meadow of Mirror Marsh, she felt eyes on her.

She had just needed to get warmed up; it was returning to her. After all those years, she had never considered herself a citizen of the Borderlands. No one decent would ever want to be associated with that term, she wouldn't have been accepted if she talked of herself that way but out in the open, walking through Mirror Marsh Jani realized she had lived wandering the Borderlands longer than she had lived her civilized, beforetimes life with Momma.

She'd missed the safety, the convenience of the beforetimes. What Momma had told her about it. Which was why despite being Commander she never volunteered to leave the gate. She left that to her crew, the Guardians who were seeking a thrill. Why she wouldn't trade the safety of their walled community for the view of an oak. Now that she was back here, whether called the Borderlands or Mirror Marsh, Jani saw she had been doing *exactly* what Momma had warned her of. Living as though she wasn't part of Mother Earth.

29: When

Prem had felt such pity for Manasa when she had read her parents' obituary. The obscenely tragic accident happening while Manasa was away from them for the first time, attending university. It had been her first and only semester. It was so unfair to Manasa. A drunk driver, in the middle of the day, caused such an accident that it was impossible for her parents to get to the lunch spot they had planned to dine at. A new tradition for them, a rekindling of their romance. A reinvestment in their marriage now that they had raised their beautiful daughter and she was off to start her own life at university. Their favorite place, their original destination had been a Greek restaurant that offered vegetarian gyros, Prem had learned when reading up on Manasa's past; an ad campaign boasting their many vegetarian options was in the paper that year.

Their daughter's life plans, not just finishing her freshman year but including attending medical school, starting her career in research, traveling across the globe to help others, continuing their family's name and legacy was all upended by a madman, her parents shot while dining at a diner close to their home, a last minute back up spot. Prem found nothing special about the restaurant, no advertisements, no menus. It wasn't around anymore and had just been a sandwich shop when it did. A place the family rarely went to. Maybe, since the restaurant's hours of operation didn't match with their schedules, maybe because Manasa's parents were like Prem's and could never justify spending money on a sandwich they could make at home. They shouldn't have been there.

These afternoon lunch dates hadn't been a possibility for Manasa's parents before. Prem had asked about it, apologizing for being so forward and Manasa had taken no offense. Riley had been at work and Prem sat on the linoleum, her notepad sliding on the kitchen floor as she took notes, the scaly skin on her neck flaking off from the extension, her ear pressing the phone into her shoulder so that her notepad didn't slide away.

When Manasa was still living with them, each hour of the day was carefully weighed and balanced, with just one car each of her parents took turns as Manasa's shuttle driver. Her parents had lived frugally and simply, saving their money for their most precious gift. Manasa was their only daughter and whatever she wanted, she got. School events, field trips, anything wholesome, educational, and affordable was encouraged by them. They gave her the childhood they wished they could have had. Prem knew they hadn't deserved to die. She cried when she had read about the accident, pulling up the story on microfiche, worried the librarians would shush her or worse, ask her what was wrong.

Prem felt an ache in her heart as she continued towards the stepwell. Look at how much fate had tried to warn them. The drunk driving accident should have told them to turn around, to go home. The roads had been closed for a reason. Their former routine was good enough. They were so close to home; couldn't they have just eaten sandwiches there? Were they punished for trying something new? How many times do we miss the signs telling us to stop, to turn around? How Manasa must have blamed herself, Prem knew she would have. Prem knew she wasn't the only one who felt she carried the entire weight of the world, the solver of all problems. How easy it was to think, and fester on, 'If only *I* had been there, I would have prevented it.' Instead of 'Why do we let people drive drunk again and again?' or 'Why did his parents buy him a gun?'

30: When

Manasa was an impressive woman, her humility intimidated Prem just as much as all that she had accomplished. Maybe these missed signs, the tragic sadness, all the what ifs fueled Manasa's urge to do good. To save her every cent. Her parents had done that for her, saved every cent they had left over. Inspired by them, their daughter did the same but with no children of her own, she chose to build a shared public water utility. Water for all beings. The madman who had murdered her parents survived and was out already, having served his time. He was no longer a threat, having killed nearly a dozen people, that was all in the past somehow. It was clear to Prem he had killed in a rage, the employee at the deli turning down an invitation after he left a generous tip. Prem read the manager refunded his entire meal, under eight dollars including the tip, and within a few minutes he returned.

And Manasa never spoke to her parents ever again.

He had been desperate, he hadn't wanted to rob the place the defense explained, he had been desperate but what else could he do? He had to eat. He had to provide. He didn't know what he was doing. And he had been so young. Lies worked, the right people believed them and ignored the outrage from the ones who did not. The young man hadn't been desperate, he had been angry. The waitress had been desperate. The customers waiting for lunch had been desperate. Manasa had known desperation. Prem did not plan to ask Manasa too much about her parents today. It was a sad story, not one to celebrate Earth Day. She refused to highlight their murderer and Heath had agreed. The article would focus on Manasa's good, and Prem thought about how she would tell her story without bringing pity into the narrative. Maybe she was making a mistake, but Prem felt it would distract from Manasa's accomplishment if Prem asked her how she managed to stay so positive after so much had been taken from her.

That did not mean that Prem did not wonder how Manasa stayed so positive. How she had gotten through those days.

31: Then

Ana had just finished reading an article on Rufus when Mr. Paisley and Wayne stepped out of Mr. Paisley's office into the reception suite. The biologists monitoring Rufus were worried he would never find love and breed. It was extremely rare that a bobcat his age wouldn't be interested in breeding, but he seemed to have no interest in looking for a mate or becoming a father.

Mr. Paisley clapped Wayne on the shoulder and called Ana into his office. Wayne winked without making eye contact with her as they passed each other; they'd decided not to let anyone at work know. It was obvious Mr. Paisley had to know. Not only did Wayne live with his brother, Willard was in charge of all the companies hirings and firings and had suggested this to Wayne and Ana, separately of course. Mr. Paisley telling Ana that he didn't want any of the other employees thinking she was on the receiving end of any favoritism. She already was allowed to use the restroom in the Executive Suite and just this past week Mr. Paisley had granted her permission to rinse the stainless-steel bottle she used for her chai in his private kitchenette. The Staff Breakroom on the main level was a mess, the sink always full of dirty dishes and the counters and floors sticky with dropped condiments and spilled sauces. She had volunteered to clean it and Mr. Paisley thanked her while also correcting her. It was best if she didn't spend too much time down there, everyone was capable of cleaning up after themselves. Ana wanted to point out that Willard seemed incapable of cleaning up after himself and realized how petty she was being. She wasn't paid to do the dishes, she was paid to be his assistant and he and Wayne had been so nice to her since she started. Ana stopped fantasizing about what it would be like if Willard was her brother-in-law one day; she and Wayne had only hung out at Kilmer's and gone out to eat a few times. And always way out of town. Wayne said he liked to drive and wanted to show her his favorite real estate locations and scout for new land with her but she couldn't help but think there was something else happening. Something that made the brothers want to keep their new love secret.

Ana settled into her seat across from Mr. Paisley and awaited his instructions. He was always sure to start with pleasantries, but Ana knew he didn't really care. It shocked her to learn he had just assigned her to the WWW Party Planning Committee, and they were meeting in a few minutes. Mr. Paisley hated last minute meetings and Ana had experienced one of his mini meltdowns just on Monday when the owner of a local gym had stopped by to discuss carrying their beverages at the gym's juice bar. Ana knew Mr. Paisley hadn't been doing anything, she still wasn't sure exactly what he did, it seemed like a lot of social calls, but had let him know the gym owner was waiting and to ask when Mr. Paisley may be able to see him.

Ana had mistakenly thought Mr. Paisley would be excited, thinking any increase in distribution meant an increase in visibility and income, but Mr. Paisley was furious that Ana had interrupted him and gave her the silent treatment the remainder of the workday. On Tuesday morning she stopped by the bakery to get him a croissant to go with his coffee and Mr. Paisley arrived acting as though nothing had happened the day before. It wasn't like Ana could have lied to the gym owner and Mr. Paisley should have been ecstatic, Ana had read the copies he had requested. The gym wanted an exclusive contract with Willard's Wellness Waters. He had gotten everything he wanted and hadn't even noticed Ana went out of the way with her apology croissant. Ana had done her job well and for some reason felt like she owed her boss an apology. Willard had thrown a temper tantrum over an unexpected meeting and was now walking her down to a meeting scheduled over her *lunch*. At that moment Ana realized how little she mattered to Mr. Paisley, he had never noticed she left her desk each day at noon to eat lunch at home, unable to afford to go out for lunch, unable to eat in the pigsty that was called the Staff Breakroom, and unable to eat in his private kitchenette or at her desk, per his own rules. Ana felt sick that she was so insignificant to him. He knew she was dating his little brother! Sort of…

Mr. Paisley provided introductions and then left. Ana had met Faith and Raven several times before; they were the only other women who worked at WWW and while Ana didn't consider them friends, she was most friendly with them. None of her other co-workers, all men, spoke with her other than a gruff greeting if Mr. Paisley scheduled a meeting with them, which was usually only if they were in some kind of trouble. Even Wayne, who she had been spending so much time with outside of work and felt had become her closest friend, didn't really acknowledge her existence when they were at work.

Since Faith worked in the Mail Room and answered the main phone at WWW, Ana saw her almost every single day. Faith had been the first to notice Ana stopped walking down to the first floor to use the ladies' room and had teased her for being so fancy. They had both laughed about how there would no longer be any reason for embarrassment when Ana ripped open tampon packaging because there was no chance anyone would hear it.

Raven had always been more serious towards Ana and Ana respected that. As the head of legal and the manager of the sales representatives, again, all men, Ana understood why Raven couldn't be seen wasting time or being a joker. Ana knew Raven worked through her lunch every day but hadn't realized she was Chair of the Party Planning Committee too.

"Did you bring your lunch Ana? We can wait to get started," Raven said as she slid a copy of the agenda across the table to Ana.

Ana shook her head no as she sat down at the conference table in front of the piece of paper.

"Well, you gotta eat," Faith advised, smiling.

"I normally eat at home," Ana began.

"I've noticed," Raven looked over to the cabinets in the conference room, "Faith, would you?"

Ana watched as Faith dragged her chair over to the cabinets on the far wall while Raven leaned over the conference table to slide Faith's takeout container towards her. Faith stood on the chair and returned to the conference table with her chair, a paper plate, and a fork.

"We don't mind eating family style," Faith mentioned as Raven made Ana a plate.

"Oh, my goodness, this is too much, I can't eat your lunches!" Ana insisted.

"It's usually too much food, anyway. You're doing us a favor," Raven tried ending the discussion curtly.

"Yeah," Faith laughed, "We don't want to store our leftovers in *that* fridge, have you seen it?"

"Yeah, it's pretty gross," Ana agreed, "I stock it every other Friday with the overage inventory."

"Yep, what an employee perk," Raven criticized flatly as she pushed Ana's plate towards her.

Ana looked at it as she didn't want to be rude and it was too late to let them know she was vegetarian. She accepted the plate and sat down next to Faith.

"I hope you like Thai food," Raven watched Ana examine her plate.

"Do you know if this has meat in it?" Ana caved and asked.

"Oh! I'm so sorry!" Raven exclaimed, "Don't eat any of the curry, the noodles are veg–do you want more? I can make you a new plate if the veg is touching the non-veg!"

"Oh no, this is great, plenty," Ana said, sincerely grateful. She hadn't eaten since breakfast.

"So, Halloween," Faith mumbled, her mouth full of curry and rice.

"Yes," Raven began, "Let's catch Ana up. Willard, er, Mr. Paisley wants us to begin planning the Halloween Party and encourage all employees to dress up."

"That sounds fun," Ana guessed.

Raven rolled her eyes and Faith laughed.

"It's a lot of work for us," Faith explained, "The sales team has a quarterly deadline that following week and will not want to waste time on-site when they should be out selling WWW."

"Maybe Mr. Paisley would push the party or the deadline if we pointed that out?" Ana asked cautiously.

"Ha!" Raven declared, "He knows. He just loves Halloween and wants to have a party."

Ana sat thoughtfully, wondering how she could make both Raven and Mr. Paisley happy. She half-listened as Faith and Raven discussed themes and catering ideas. As the end of their lunch hour neared, Raven asked Ana if she had any questions or needed any other information before they wrapped up for the week.

"Well, I was wondering, what if we invite some of the sales reps or even Wayne to be on the committee or to take on some of the planning? Maybe if they're involved, there will be more excitement and less pressure on us to make sure everyone attends and shows Mr. Paisley they're having a good time?"

Raven tossed her takeout container into the trash and told Ana Wayne *was* on the Party Planning Committee. Ana looked to Faith as though she couldn't believe Raven was telling the truth, if Wayne was on the committee, where was he?

"You don't really expect the boss's brother to spend his lunch hour with the Party Planning Committee, do you Ana?" Faith quizzed as though it should be obvious.

Ana had nothing to say to that, she figured once Wayne knew she served on the Party Planning Committee too, he'd start attending. She stood, placed her plate in the trash and followed Faith out of the conference room.

"One more thing Ana," Raven stalled. Ana watched as Faith waved goodbye with her palm and then walked towards the mailroom.

"What's up?" Ana asked eagerly, hoping she could help Raven, so she didn't feel so burdened.

"Don't worry about lunch next week, we'll order."

"Oh, I'll bring my lunch, I'm saving money still," Ana shared cautiously. Raven was always so put together and Ana didn't want to look poor to her. She wished she could dress as well as Raven who always wore heels and had her hair and nails done. Ana knew Raven had to get up hours before Mr. Paisley, Wayne, or any of the men she supervised, just to look 'professional'.

"Don't worry about it. Consider it a treat from Faith and me."

"We've got a lot of meetings before Halloween. The cost will add up. I can't take advantage of you both like this."

"Listen Ana, I understand your caution. You won't owe us any favors. I promise. The Party Planning Committee receives a budget from Mr. Paisley each quarter and Faith and I figure if we aren't getting paid during our lunch hour, Mr. Paisley can at least buy us lunch."

Ana considered this and then finally nodded. She understood what Raven meant. There were a lot of little things Ana did for Willard and Wayne, who wasn't even her boss. They weren't in her job description and Mr. Paisley probably wouldn't even notice unless she stopped doing them. Like trying to make him feel happy with her fake positive attitude, getting the fancier cheese and fruit from the store for his business 'meetings', and letting him slap her ass every once in a while.

32: When

On her own Prem had become familiar with the work Manasa did after she dropped out of university, administrative jobs, often supplemented with work as a nanny. Manasa often had roommates; Prem had learned from their talks on the phone all the ways Manasa was frugal so she didn't have to touch the savings her parents had left behind.

Of all the menial office jobs Manasa had held, mailroom clerk, receptionist, photocopier aide, Prem had fixated on Manasa's time with a now defunct wellness promotions company, where she had for a very short time been the executive assistant to *the* Willard Paisley, who over the past few years had become quite wealthy through real estate investment properties and in Prem's opinion tax evasion. When she had learned of the connection, she had felt a pain in her stomach. It was no wonder Manasa rarely left her home in the marsh, Prem could only imagine how much pain those billboards brought her. Paisley was someone who took and took and everything Prem had learned about Manasa was that she had felt loss again and again.

There had been buzz for a while that he'd be running for Governor or maybe even for a seat in the House, in a few years. Prem looked into Paisley's wellness promotions company and found little. It had had little success although he hit the market early, selling tonics and energy drinks to local gyms, dance, and yoga studios. Drinks which Paisley claimed gave you energy and fought off fat. Prem knew water did just the same thing, but Paisley had the foresight and the capital and as demand grew, he didn't want to keep up with the production of these wellness tonics and the regulation that was being demanded. No, he would not involve himself in any sort of regulation, so when Paisley had the chance, he sold the company and kept the property. Rinse and repeat to make his riches, wherever his hobbies led him, there was money to be made and land to be bought.

Manasa had only been with him for short term employment. Prem imagined they didn't keep in touch.

Isolated in Mirror Marsh Prem found it hard to imagine anyone keeping in touch with Manasa.

33: When

Prem noticed the change in terrain when the song of Mirror Marsh changed, muted from the muddy bank and yet louder as the tune echoed off the stone pavilion.

"It'll be much nicer once all the vegetation has grown back," Manasa said as she offered a smile to Prem, "It will make it safer to walk through but for now the earth must heal from the construction equipment we rented to create the stepwell. Here, allow me."

Prem accepted Manasa's extended hand, commenting on her mehndi, "Did someone get married?"

"Oh, this?" Manasa took her hand back and displayed both palms, "Special occasion. Auspicious event."

Prem held on to her fingertips, admiring the design, "Whoa! Are these snakes?"

"Look closely," Manasa said before raising her hands to the heavens and spinning just as Prem had. Prem noticed the designs in nature, replicated in the stone of the stepwell around her, amazed how they matched the designs in Manasa's mehndi. Prem hadn't expected such detail, such an elegant design. And as always, Manasa denied it was anything special, that she had created this all herself.

The two women walked slowly down the muddy path towards the stone pavers signaling the entrance to the stepwell.

"This is absolutely magnificent!" Prem exclaimed as she took her tiny steps, stopping to turn as she caught the design on the walkways and walls, and wishing she could take a photo of Manasa's hands to compare, "I cannot believe you didn't let us bring a photographer!"

"Us?" Manasa worried, stopping in her tracks.

"Yeah, us, the paper," Prem realizing she may have caused offense.

"Are others coming?" Manasa asked, upsetting Prem with the change in her tone.

Prem was unnerved, her stomach sunk. She shook her head and wondered if Manasa knew about her camera.

"No photos!" Manasa called before playfully leading the way ahead.

34: Now

When Jani first arrived at the Deer Commons gatehouse, she had been running from trying to survive on her own, the only outside help was that which Mother Earth offered. She had expected to be shot, Momma had always warned her, and Jani was ready to die when she first saw the structure, the potential behind those walls after being on her own for too long, Jani had been ready to walk right up to the gates before remembering what Momma had taught her. *Scout first, then plan.*

On the emptiest of stomachs, Jani had climbed to the highest ground she could find to learn what existed within their walls. She munched on the wild grasses growing on the hillside she had found, spitting out the roughest of the roughage. Jani munched, waited, and watched and saw nothing that should scare her off. Of course, the only thing she saw of value for the two nights she sheltered on that hillside was that no one ever left the gates. But Jani had heard not one scream, nor one gun shot. Momma had taught her boring could mean safety and boring could also mean no power, *there are men that want to control you Jani, don't you ever forget. If they can't manipulate you, they'll force you.*

After two days of eating mainly grass Jani was running out of water rations so made the decision to approach the people who lived within those walls, a decision she may not have made if she wasn't so young and so hungry. Momma had told her there was safety in numbers, but that madness laid there too.

Jani slept well in her hidden shelter on the hill and then when she woke, well before daybreak, she began courageously making her way towards Deer Commons. She scooted down the hill on her bottom until finally the sky started to turn grey, Surya having jumped over the horizon.

Sounding out the words, *Deer Commons*, Jani walked the paved path towards the gate. The residents were still maintaining the path and Jani saw their metal signage wasn't terribly worn down or covered in obscene graffiti but cared for with pride, she had wanted to run her hands across it, it was just like the beforetimes with Momma. Momma always tried to bring Jani to places like this, something outside of their world for Jani to aspire towards.

Jani walked a steady pace past the sign adorned with deer, rabbits, and a raccoon frolicking together across a meadow, something Jani had never seen in her years of traveling across the wilderness of the Borderlands. Just like in all the tales Momma told, the animals on the sign to Deer Commons seemed to have a better handle on friendship than humans and Jani liked that about them, even if she'd never witnessed it. She wanted to believe they looked out for each other, went out of their way to help.

Familiar with the other sign, hanging on intervals as she approached the gatehouse, Jani read the words as an inner monologue, *NO TRESPASSING*. The signs with camera on them, *Say Cheese, you're on camera!* Momma hadn't been able to explain that one, cheese was something everyone had liked, being cheesy, however Jani's mind couldn't quite expand to understand why cheese.

Jani didn't read so well back then but she still had the basics down. Momma used everything she could to educate her daughter, she had made sure Jani could sound out the words *Deer Commons* when she saw them. But reading that word, sounding it out, knowing she was being watched as she did so, *cheese*, made Jani feel small, stupid, like she should just turn around. She would just be a burden, why would they accept another mouth to feed?

Jani adjusted rapidly to her change in environment after she was welcomed past the gatehouse. She'd heard the argument: *it's on Myles if it turns out she's feral*. After her quarantine she had seen him again, met with The Council. She was quiet, and they had liked that. Myles had told her to be cautious, prophesying that the less Jani said, the less Jani could mess up.

It was not the luxurious world Momma had described when telling her stories of Kings and Queens (only to teach her the difference between Queens and Knights) but every single thing in Deer Commons felt very lavish to Jani. She was in a brand-new world. Everyone in Deer Commons had clothes that were always so clean. Jani saw so many people helping, taking care of things Momma had never even talked about.

Four days after she had been granted entrance by Commander Myles, she gradually opened up to the idea that they really wanted her to stay there and help them. That nothing bad was going to happen. Contemplating her new reality of living safely within the walls of Deer Commons she had asked Reba Auntie about the trails within their stone walls, in awe of the kilometers of forested walking trails, where residents could go on walks for *leisure. Was it safe?*

"I understand why you worry but you don't need to. We've got Guardians. Oh, those are mainly junk trees," Reba Auntie casually responded, changing the subject before listing out the most common trees as they walked, "Silver maple, sugar maple, we keep trying to grow some elms although they don't get too big."

Reba Auntie told Jani about the invasive disease that plagued the elms yet how they kept trying to survive in Deer Commons. Many little sprouts growing into seedlings and then saplings but once they matured problems set in. The Arborists worked hard to protect these mature elms, to help them survive and grow strong, deep into Mother Earth as much as towards the unknown of the sky, if successful, creating the shape of a fan and providing much shade for the villagers. But only the Arborists could go near them, a strictly enforced protocol, changing their uniforms and shoes to prevent transmitting the disease to the elms living their whole lives in isolation. Reba Auntie explained that if they could ever get a grove of them, they would be able to rely on the timber sourced for repairs around the village, for furniture, and maybe even one day, they'd have a renewable source for paper, returning to a practice their people had once had. Jani had never heard of a Scriptorium before then. Every day she was learning unfamiliar words, mad at herself for being mad at her Momma for not providing them to her.

Jani wondered if the elms in Deer Commons had ever spread a message from their roots to any of the trees here in Mirror Marsh.

35: When

Prem thought of their conversations on the phone as she saw Manasa waiting for Prem to catch up, leaning on a pillar just as Prem had leaned against their kitchen wall. When Prem caught up, she took in the intricate detail of the pillars decorated with vines and flowers. Manasa posed with a playful smile; her hands postured on the pillars to show off the designs.

Prem planned to sketch as much as she could and began wondering whether it would be ok for her to ask Manasa to take a photo. Prem gently waved her spiral-bound notebook, hoping she could make a quick sketch now, but Manasa's eyes expressed annoyance while her actions were playful; she smacked the small notepad out of Prem's loose grip and the two women watched as it tumbled to the ground.

Prem stood there until Manasa giggled and Prem shocked herself by giggling in response, then apologizing as she bent down to retrieve her notebook. As they walked, she expressed her admiration for the designs selected to Manasa.

Manasa offered no response and did not seem concerned when Prem began running her fingers across the cool stone, feeling the detailed craftwork. This had not been DIYed. Just as with Manasa's mehndi some were not vines at all but snakes and flowers, but where there was enough light, Prem saw some held messages within. Prem's heart quickened but not from fear. She was excited to be in this strange place making these bizarre discoveries.

Manasa returned to Prem's side from the shadows, when she saw Prem was no longer with her. She watched Prem as she traced her fingertip along the script in stone.

"Have you read this one?" Prem inquired.

"I have read them all."

"*Let it be known that Monika and Poonam light up my every morning,*" Prem read to Manasa, "This is *so* sweet!"

"I hope you get to see my favorite," Manasa replied.

Prem noticed a light flash in the corner of her eyes as Manasa led Prem through from the outdoor pavilion towards the stairs leading to the indoor pavilion.

"Just the first of many steps for you Prem," Manasa said as she gestured for Prem to go ahead. Prem began climbing and then doubled back down the cool stone steps after hearing Manasa sing her name.

Prem thought she knew the tune, humming it as she marched back, feeling a rush when she found Manasa crouching, balancing on her toes as she laid her mehndied palm on one of the stones.

"Can you read this?" Manasa asked as she leaned down to sit on the steps.

"I think so, it's a little dark," Prem mused as she traced the design on the stone.

"Yeah, the light plays tricks always but especially here."

"Did *you* carve all of these stones?"

"That's part of your interview, you would tell me if we'd begun," Manasa warbled loudly before whispering, "Molds and tools, not everything is *stone* stone, natural. Some bricks are manmade."

Prem felt the vibration of Manasa's words in the stairwell and opened her mouth to ask another question, but Manasa spoke again, over her, almost bellowing, "Let me read it. Here," Manasa squeezed in, forcing Prem to walk backwards up the steps otherwise touch her bare skin. "*All shall know that Manasa used the might of her life to build these steps. Respect them and walk through this monument with care or be advised to move along. Far, far away from here.*"

Prem chuckled nervously, "That is pretty cute."

"Cute. I was going for haunting," Manasa raised her eyebrows before jokingly laughing like an evil villain.

Prem chuckled too and Manasa placed her hand on Prem's bare shoulder. Prem held her breath, hoping the dimness hid her dermatological issues.

Prem wondered what Manasa was thinking as they stood together, skin to skin.

Manasa squeezed her shoulder and moved up the steps and Prem felt a breeze touch her skin only where Manasa's hand had been.

36: When

"We saved a stone for you to inscribe. You'll let the engineers know what you'd like inscribed. You, not the paper," Manasa emphasized.

Prem raised her eyebrows in surprise and looked up asking, "I thought the stepwell was complete?"

"Oh, it is," Manasa released her hand and waved it dismissively, "I just thought this would, like be a fun part of your interview!"

"Okay," Prem said cautiously, wondering to herself when she would have time to think of something timeless, meaningful. She was a writer and these words would be left behind forever, inscribed in stone, as though she was an ancient being, not a modern one.

Manasa and Prem continued climbing and soon they stood together on the platform, as they emerged from the stairwell Prem saw the space was almost entirely empty, with a slightly less open space framed by two stone benches and a stone throne. Prem followed Manasa, expecting her to settle into the throne but instead Manasa gestured widely before settling onto one of the two benches on either side of the throne. Prem felt ridiculous sitting on the throne or the floor so selected the bench directly across from Manasa. As she set her tote bag down next to her, she noticed how simple the benches were when compared to the throne, which was elaborately decorated with lotus flowers and serpents, some of which were sticking out their forked tongues.

Prem saw similarities of this pattern from the design of Manasa's mehndi except with Manasa's throne, all the snakes had their eyes on Prem, she truly felt they were watching her. It took everything in her power to hold back her laughter and she wondered if Manasa had really been joking about haunting the halls of the stepwell one day.

Jani had been successful in tracking, walking Drishti's same route, until she had gotten to Hell's Hill. At that point, it was as though Drishti had entirely disappeared. Jani refused to give up, Drishti could awaken the serpents, giving them more power. Jani could not give up, the village was already weakened. The serpents had bitten many. There was no way to get rid of them. If Drishti spoke of Deer Commons, if the cultists came there, Jani was not sure how much of Deer Commons could survive.

She had found signs of Drishti as she moved through the meadow but those signs didn't actually mean it was Drishti. It could very well be one of the cultists of Mirror Marsh, abandoning Drishti's things, creating a false trail. Leading Jani into a trap.

This was exactly why The Council secretly enforced this law, it was a bigger danger for a citizen to leave their walls more than it had been letting one, naïve and ignorant young girl in. No one in Deer Commons was a prisoner, if you asked to leave, the villagers would be sad to see you go but you were free to do so. The Council would even send you out the gate with a pack filled with a few things to help on your journey.

She had been eager to please The Council. She didn't question them, ask to see the law in the Scriptorium, where all records were kept. She had understood her responsibility. The secret mission assigned to her. As Commander of the Guardians Jani had watched The Council send just one villager off, Jeff Uncle. She had liked him. When she had first moved in with Reba Auntie sometimes the landowners would stare, whisper. Never Jeff Uncle. He always waved, scooted over for her and Reba Auntie to join him. Reba Auntie had told her it had happened twice before, both neighbours, years apart, believed the world was safe again, wanted to see for themselves. Myles hadn't ever spoken of this part of the job.

It was a secret yet still, parents hushed children to never even wonder, *what's outside*? Each time there was a big send off, a banquet dinner to honor the villager they had lost, the citizen's accomplishments toasted by all. But no excitement of a new day, all the possibilities. No requests to come back to Deer Commons, to share the news of the outside world, before they left the gate. The villagers did not know The Council did so much to keep them safe. They just worried what evil might come to their gate if the wrong people found their neighbor, outside their walls. The

Council believed there was only one bigger threat to Deer Commons than outsiders and that was letting people who knew the wealth of Deer Commons out into the Borderlands. What would happen if they were desperate.

She still couldn't believe Myles had let her in. That he had fought for her. That Myles had known.

38: When

The platform reminded Prem of her childhood family room, except instead of couches set in a U shape to give everyone sight of a television, their outdoor living room had a direct view to the stepwell below. Prem feared the height of where she was and the depth of the pool below. It was so eerie looking to her, a few dozen steps leading down to where? How deep was the water, freshwater fed from the watershed of the Marigold River, topped off by the natural cycles of rainwater and contained by Manasa's creation.

Prem held back a shiver thinking of the unknown depth of the stepwell, considering that she was being nervous, silly and superstitious. Nevertheless, when she had walked past it, she had almost heard a voice, a feeling so strong telling her it was best to not stand too close to the edge. Prem felt the giggles percolate to the surface again, imagining an uncontrollable laughter as she jumped off the edge. She wouldn't have to worry about the drive home in the dark then. All by herself. There was a railing but nothing to stop Prem from standing on it. Prem couldn't believe the pull she felt to look out over the edge again.

Prem pretended to go through her bag, telling herself that a backyard pool in Deer Commons was probably more dangerous than this manmade oasis. Manasa had referred to it being manmade, using manmade materials but had clarified she wanted to make sure Prem wrote down that women had built it. Prem had made a note in her reporter's notebook when she said that, scribbling a reminder to bring this angle into her story for Heath not knowing if the investors would be okay with publishing it. Sisters saving Mother Earth, Prem jotted down, words to prevent her brain from thinking about the depth of the well, the pool which couldn't be contained by the Marigold River beneath her.

39: When

Manasa declared she was ready to begin, and Prem scribbled as she spoke, noticing how the ink of her lucky pen matched the darkness of the pool in the stepwell.

Prem wanted to hold Manasa's gaze but felt unsettled by the strength behind her eyes, the command Manasa held always caused Prem to glance away.

Just as she had been on the phone, Prem was captured by every word Manasa spoke. Manasa was just a few years older than Prem but Prem felt as though she was in proximity to an elder. Only Prem's elders were not quite as supportive as Manasa seemed to be. Prem's worries that she wouldn't be able to ask Manasa questions respectfully left her mind. She could see the respect Manasa saw others with; all beings her equal. She commanded the space but did not do so with authority, other than the authority she had over herself. Prem kicked herself for making such assumptions about another woman, especially when she had felt the weight of assumptions herself. To reject the hierarchy of South Asian culture wasn't something Prem had witnessed. Walking alone through adulthood as Manasa had was something Prem had never witnessed either. Manasa was only intimidating to Prem because Prem had experienced no one like Manasa before.

"Chai?" Manasa asked.

"Really?" Prem asked back, surprised at the offer.

Manasa laughed, "If it wasn't for chai would we ever get anything done? Look under your bench."

Prem laughed politely, not quite understanding Manasa's quip, "Wow, thank you," Prem stumbled, reaching for the stainless-steel bottle under her bench as her notepad and pen dropped on the stone floor, next to her feet.

"Prem," Manasa began, "Take a breath. You seem to be a bundle of nerves. Please, take your time. I promise I am in no rush and I'm sorry if I rushed you by announcing I was ready to begin."

Prem sat embarrassed, she had picked her belongings up and felt that she had ruined the interview before it even began, thinking she must look so *weak* to Manasa.

Manasa smiled, "I promise. We really have no rush. Whenever you're ready."

"I'm getting close!" Prem said brightly. She could fake having her shit together, just like Riley said to. She fished the tape recorder out of her tote bag and showed it to Manasa and Manasa nodded in understanding. Prem hit the little red circle, creating a record of the people in this large stone creation.

"So, we are here to hear the story of my stepwell?" Manasa asked.

"Yes, we can begin anywhere. I always like to start with the basics, who you are, where you're from. Then we can move on to your expertise or anything else you'd want to share about bringing the public here, how your work celebrates Earth Day, benefits the planet, all that."

"Yes, but first," Manasa said soothingly, raising her own stainless-steel bottle in a toast, "Chai?"

"To chai!" Prem said, a chill running over her skin again. Just that crazy feeling she always had that was wrong. She tried calming herself by saying all she needed to do was call for help and began spiraling as she jumped to the thought of the distance to the nearest phone to call for help, it wouldn't be Manasa's cottage but why would she even need to call for help? Nothing had even happened.

"Shall we then?" Manasa snapped Prem back to reality.

Prem looked at her recorder and watched the tape coiling, "So, a stepwell. In Mirror Marsh. Where should we even begin?"

Manasa tilted her head and professed, "It was important to my parents I learn Sanskrit. That languages were only lost when the stories that held their words were. In some ways it was easy to learn, in others not so much. They taught me the word *jeevan,* it had many meanings, one was life, and another was water. That our ancestors understood that water equates life. For all beings."

40: Then

Ana dressed the salad and made plates for Faith and Raven before making herself one and joining them at the conference room table. Raven was very frustrated at Paisley's insistence on a costume contest. Halloween was on a Friday this year and Raven had wanted to take a half day at work so she could attend her children's Halloween Parade at their elementary school.

"I know I'm not the only one," Raven vented, "I'm already being so lazy buying my kids their costumes. Charlie's been making me feel so terrible, but I don't have time to do everything. I barely get enough sleep and now I have to make my *own* costume?"

"I know what you mean, I can't afford to buy a costume really. I've been helping my sister and her husband out a lot and things are tight right now. He was injured and isn't cleared to return full time," Faith disclosed.

"Okay, so what's a costume that might be really easy to put together?" Ana began before answering her own question, "Witch! Witches! Everyone can put together an all-black costume, right? We can grab broom sticks from the supply closet! Or make wands out of anything, use old sticks we find on the ground?"

Ana watched as Raven and Faith looked at one another across the conference table.

"I don't know how the men would feel about our suggestion they dress as witches," Raven cautioned.

"Fine," Ana said, "Tell them witches or wizards, same thing isn't it? Just one seems smarter?"

"Not bad," Faith admitted.

"I'll let Mr. Paisley know when we meet in the morning," Raven made a note on the agenda.

"Awesome!" Ana exclaimed, "Now on to selecting our catering!"

41: When

Prem shifted her weight, the stone bench had grown incredibly uncomfortable under her bottom. She continued scribbling as she thought about how these benches were for brief rests and her worry grew, Manasa had seemed so fun on the phone and here in Mirror Marsh, in the stepwell she felt off. Different.

On the phone Prem had loved hearing her stories, Manasa's wisdom traveling through the spiraling phone cord but sitting across from one another on these benches, Manasa sipping her chai from a wide mouthed bottle and Prem from her narrow one, Manasa no longer sounded like a philanthropist or even an eco-warrior like Heath had warned. So far Manasa's monologue was a defamation suit waiting to happen, Prem understood the animosity, especially with those awful billboards but that hadn't been what Manasa was going on and on about. Prem also understood that Paisley had to have been an awful boss but thought Manasa was pretty petty for working for a family business and expecting to be treated as though you were your boss's family.

Prem hadn't given up though, she was just thinking that Manasa was out of her mind if she thought the *Gazette* would stand up to the Paisley boys. Looking down at where her pen met the paper, Prem hoped her face did not show the concern she had for her safety. How upset would Manasa get if Prem suggested a tour. Maybe walked Manasa out to her cottage and then took some photos on the way back to Riley's truck. Manasa did not sound well at all, and Prem was disappointed with herself for running away with a fantasy before she really got to know her. The turning point came when after several attempts to get Manasa to speak to the significance of the stepwell she had finally held up her hand in anger, Prem wondering how Manasa got henna as she watched her outstretched palm shake, commanding Prem to listen and learn the truth.

And so, Prem sat and listened to Manasa's diatribe about her former employer. None of it was surprising, but it all seemed very petty. Prem flipped a page in her notebook and began a list of questions for the civil engineers, they were experts on sustainability and she could probably get a pretty good draft ready for Heath if she could extract herself from Manasa's grasp.

Prem had almost completely filled the page when she realized Manasa had stopped talking. She glanced up, faking an eager look upon her face, not wanting to upset Manasa further as she had noticed her once open palms were now clenched in fists.

A raven landed on the railing, and Manasa spoke to it, "You were right, they wanted to report on something cheerful, and I went on for too long about my terrible employer and I no longer look like a shero."

Prem moved her focus to the large black bird, watching them pick through their feathers with their beak as Manasa continued, "I just wanted her to understand these relationships, we are all connected."

Prem nodded in understanding and saw the raven did too.

42: When

She wanted to tell Manasa that she had also suffered, complete strangers asking her about her own adoption. Not caring about her feelings, just satisfying their own curiosity of whether or not Prem was grateful. Total strangers talking to a child about nature versus nurture and how bad her life would have been otherwise. The interview was about Manasa, but Manasa had paused, allowing Prem to feel her anger. Testing Prem before she continued.

43: Now

Jani worried if Hans would ever find out. He knew her responsibility. That she hadn't done what she needed to do. She had found Jeff Uncle quickly; he was old and had no experience journeying through the wild terrain that surrounded Deer Commons. She had woken him gently, misery in her chest when she found him, he hadn't even set up a warning to wake him if predators got near, he hadn't slept with a weapon nearby. Jeff Uncle had smiled when he saw Jani, the corners wilting as she explained. She wouldn't kill him, but they would if he ever returned to Deer Commons. She did what The Council would not. Begged him to not speak of Deer Commons to anyone he came across. And then she took the sack full of provisions that he clutched, tugging it from his grasp.

Jani had not killed him, but she had left him in the Borderlands with nothing but the clothes on his back.

Hans had hugged her and cried when she returned to the gate, holding Jeff Uncle's sack. Proof to The Council that she had done her job. That Deer Commons would be safe.

44: Then

"I'm really excited, I have no idea where you're taking me," Ana slid into the bucket seat next to Wayne.

"Me too babe. You're about to witness my dream," Wayne trumpeted before he kissed her passionately.

Ana had never driven the route Wayne was taking. Although Ana and Wayne had lived relatively close to one another Ana was not particularly familiar with much of the state. Her parents tended to either keep very close to home or travel halfway across the world to their other home, always for their research.

Ana enjoyed the scenic drive and feeling Wayne's arm slung around her shoulders. She didn't mind that they couldn't be seen together like she had at first. Once she understood how awkward that would be for Mr. Paisley, she could accept it a little. But learning how much Raven and Faith despised Wayne made *Ana* want to keep their romance a secret. Wayne had no clue how much they disliked him. Ana had told him how his brother had appointed her on the Party Planning Committee and all he had done was laugh and then kiss her neck, completely ignoring her work update.

"Everything okay Ana?"

Ana realized she was gripping Wayne's leg, "I'm so sorry. I guess these dirt roads and the steep climb are more thrilling than I realized."

"You really have no idea," Wayne laughed again before pressing on the gas and speeding up up the steep hill.

Ana had to force herself to breathe, she had never witnessed Wayne acting so recklessly before. Ana was worried they were going to tip off the side of the hill, if anything came in Wayne's path he would be driving too fast to stop.

"We're here!" Wayne called before swerving to the side of the hill and abruptly braking.

"Whoa!" Ana said as she collected herself, telling herself that she'd put her seatbelt on for the drive home, even if it meant not sitting so close to Wayne.

"C'mon, I can't wait to show you!"

Ana slid across the seat and grabbed Wayne's extended hand. He pulled her towards him and kissed her before dragging her further up the hill.

"Hang on! I'm not wearing the best shoes for this!" Ana exclaimed as she tried to keep her wedges on her feet.

"Alright," Wayne said before sweeping Ana off her feet to carry her.

"Oh my God Wayne!" Ana squealed.

"We're here!" Wayne set Ana down on her feet and kissed her gently.

"And what is this?" Ana asked. All she could see was the marshy earth below the peak of the hill.

"You'll never guess but try. I'll give you three of 'em," Wayne teased.

Ana didn't know what to guess. She wanted to believe maybe he was going to propose to her but knew that couldn't be; she still hadn't told him so much and there was so much she didn't know about him.

"I dunno. It's a marsh so maybe we're going on an adventure? To see some wildlife?"

"Ana," Wayne said condescendingly, "You're never going to guess so I'll just tell you. You're looking at my first investment property!"

Ana looked at Wayne, waiting for his explanation.

"Okay, fine, we will get back in the car so you can see all the critters in the marsh. Just don't complain about it being their home, I know what a hippie dippie you are about loving the animals and not eating them," Wayne lectured, "You're looking at my first property—Paisley's Private Landfill!"

"What?" Ana was confused.

"I've got a bit more to save but Pa agreed with my first investment. If I buy this land, intending to turn it into a landfill, he will help me with the business side. Set up some contracts with the city to dump here!" Wayne picked Ana up, this time to swing her around.

"Oh, that's great. I'm happy for you," Ana lied. She thought Wayne was interested in buying properties and renting them out and hadn't thought about how land could be rented in other ways.

As they drove down the hill towards the marsh Wayne didn't even notice Ana was no longer sitting under his arm. She felt so much safer buckled in, even at the slower speed Wayne was driving at. She listened to him brag about how smart his father had called him, in front of Willard. She heard him talk about how much more money he would make than his older brother but could only think of the marsh being filled with waste. She knew it wasn't the most beautiful place to visit but it was so important for the health of their ecosystem. For the planet.

Wayne held Ana's hand as they stomped through the tall grasses. Ana thought about how Wayne hadn't really even stopped to include Ana in this conversation, he had just been lecturing her about how rich this was going to make him and how stupid Willard would look in ten years.

Ana heard something and stopped in her tracks, refusing to budge even when Wayne tugged on her hand.

"Hold up, do you hear that?" Ana asked.

Wayne and Ana stood listening to the wind blow through the grasses of the marsh, Wayne had almost lost his patience with Ana when he heard it too, the slight rattle sound.

"Where is it?" Wayne shouted.

"Calm down!" Ana tried to say gently, "He's warning us, he wants us to stay away, he doesn't want to hurt us!"

Ana watched in horror as Wayne started sweeping the grasses with his hands, looking for the rattlesnake.

"That's it, I'm leaving," Ana turned around to walk back to Wayne's car.

Wayne didn't follow her, and she sat on the hood of his vehicle hoping he hadn't gotten bit. She had family who had died this way, her parents had told her so, and that was what drove their research. Despite knowing a universal anti-venom would never be created in their lifetimes, they still attempted to find one.

She cupped her hands over her eyes as she noticed Wayne returning to where he had parked his car. He seemed to be walking just fine. As he got closer, he began to run and Ana saw he was grinning almost ear to ear. He jumped on the hood and slid across it, almost bumping Ana off.

"Whoa," he sang as he grabbed her around the waist, "Okay, guess what I saw!"

"The snake?" Ana guessed.

"Oh! I forgot about that!" Wayne laughed, "That was real good of you Ana, you've got ears! No! I didn't see the snake, but I saw two cranes! I'm gonna take Pa here and we'll hunt 'em! Once the land is mine of course."

Wayne leaned over and kissed Ana, high off the excitement he was feeling. All the riches that were headed his way. Ana kissed him back but then pushed him away.

"We should probably get going, don't want to drive back in pitch dark and all," Ana suggested.

"You're right, as usual babe," Wayne said with a wink.

As they got ready to leave Wayne asked Ana to sit next to him and she hesitated but then did as he asked. It was a long drive back to her apartment and it would be too awkward if she refused. She decided she would instead say something if she felt he was driving recklessly.

Wayne started the car and then turned to her, kissing her passionately once again. Ana let him as she had nowhere to go. Wayne held her shoulders so she was turned to face him.

"I'm going to say something, and I know it's going to sound crazy, but I think I love you Ana," Wayne panted before pulling her close and kissing her again.

Wayne didn't wait for a response after he pulled away from their kiss, turning to start the drive back home. He rolled down the windows and screamed and Ana laughed. It made her happy to see Wayne so happy.

They listened to the tunes on the radio and sang along. As they got closer to the city and Ana's apartment it was as though Wayne remembered Ana was part of their date too.

"Hey," Wayne began, "Weren't you going to tell me about your name Ahhh-naa?"

Ana smiled, "Wow, that was a few weeks back, wasn't it? Well, my full name is Manasa, I've been going by Ana since I was in school, was always easier than teaching people how to pronounce my full name."

Wayne tried pronouncing it and Ana laughed, telling him, "Exactly."

"So, what does that mean? You're an ass to a man?" Wayne laughed at himself.

Ana explained Manasa Devi to Wayne, she had been waiting to tell him how both her parents had siblings who had been bit by snakes but through prayer survived. How her parents knew prayer to Nagini wasn't enough, but science was there to help. How they had named her after Manasa Devi because they knew the importance of snakes in maintaining nature's biodiversity as frightening as snakes may be. Except Wayne changed the subject to what interested him.

"Yeah, you made the right choice going with Ahh-naaa. Much easier to pronounce than, what was it? Sexy snake lady?"

"Hilarious. No, my parents wanted to be sure other kids could pronounce my name and then it just kind of stuck."

"I get that," Wayne related, "My Pa always calls me Eddie, but I like Wayne," Wayne interrupted himself, "You'll be my sexy snake lady then, right? Are you still scared of your landlord finding out or are you finally ready for me to slither into your bed?"

45: When

Prem noticed the shadows on the platform had shifted. As she watched Manasa gulp her chai Prem noted a reminder to bring a metaphor of a dirty sink to her story; the stepwell and Mirror Marsh had been so close to becoming a landfill.

Manasa stood and looked over the edge of the platform. Prem watched her look down and frown as she shook her bottle, judging how much chai she had left.

46: When

Prem coughed and shook her own bottle, offering it to Manasa when she looked over. Manasa shook her head no and then took her hand, covered in mehndi, and laid it on top of her own chai bottle. Prem took a sip of her own chai understanding Manasa wanted no more.

Manasa stared straight ahead; above the stepwell she had created. Prem stood in the silence and stretched her sore muscles, she had never liked silence, but she knew that leaving space for subjects to speak without prodding, often resulted in the best stories.

"You don't smoke, do you Prem?" Manasa probed.

"I have and I don't," Prem admitted to Manasa asking back, "How about you?"

Manasa laughed, "Such a nasty habit. Nails for your coffin!"

"If we use coffins," Prem swore she heard Manasa flatly say, telling herself if Manasa hadn't gone into such detail, she'd have captured it on her recording.

Manasa sounded exhausted, "Bad for the health of all, the smoker, the beings around the smoker, the litter it causes. Did you know they don't decompose for decades? I can't believe it is legal to destroy Mother Earth like this!"

Prem watched Manasa take a deep breath. "I'm sorry," she apologized as she leaned over the edge.

Prem walked towards her and noticed the tears in Manasa's eyes, knowing there were so many possibilities that could have caused this outburst.

47: Now

With all the secrets they kept from one another, why not? What trust could Drishti have left in her elders?

Drishti hadn't gone to The Council, sought permission from them, explained her reasoning for wanting to leave the gates. Just as the serpents had appeared in Deer Commons, suddenly, out of nowhere, Drishti had somehow escaped.

She didn't want to believe how Drishti had gotten out but there could only be one answer. As Jani focused on tracking Drishti, she had realized Hans had helped Drishti leave, she had woken up alone in the Command Station but hadn't thought twice about what time Hans had left.

He had asked her something strange that night, Jani had completely forgotten. Jani had been standing at their map of Deer Commons, her index finger on the Scriptorium. The Council had told her it was of utmost importance to keep the serpents out of the kitchens and the Scriptorium.

She had thought he was joking. Hans never joked. He had pulled her finger off the map and kissed it before asking, "Do you ever wonder if there's any truth behind the Legend of Eadwayne?"

48: When

Prem didn't know how long they had been standing looking over the stepwell in silence. Manasa looked at her chai before saying, "I made this chai. The sun will be setting before we know it, to my last cup."

Prem thought it sounded as though Manasa had slurred as she spoke those words.

49: When

"Did you know we are made to look out for them? To always be aware?"

Prem had been listening to Manasa lecture on serpents and the rock rattlesnake's importance in the ecosystem of Mirror Marsh and it was all being wasted. Manasa half clung to Prem in the stairwell's darkness, every once in a while a sliver of light reflected in somehow and Prem had noticed how Manasa traced the snakes just how Prem did. Self-soothing sensations.

The lecture was wasted, Prem's cassettes were full, and it was much too dark to write in the stairwell, even if Manasa hadn't been leaning on her.

"I watched as our gaze grew further and further away," Manasa continued her inebriated oration, "Our dependence on needing and wanting more led to us ignoring all that we have. These idiots want to sell us bottled water now! Consume, consume, consume. Purchasing is your right. That's what this has to do with the stepwell. I wanted to build a place where all could congregate. Stop and fill your container! Why must we create so much waste? Someone has to try. We all must try to help each other, all living beings. The time is being forced upon us, by those who seek power. It will hurt and we must return to living with the land, not exploiting it!"

Prem gently guided Manasa down the stairs. If she hadn't gotten to know her through their talks over the phone, Prem wouldn't let Manasa near her.

Manasa sounded like a madwoman. One incident of not quite sexual harassment made her sound like a super villain when she got drunk. Manasa even sounded to Prem like a doomsday cult leader, the kind that kills everyone whether or not they were her followers.

Lost in her thoughts Prem didn't notice Manasa slip her now empty bottle of chai into her tote bag.

Prem had come here for a feel-good news story and the feel-good part had yet to come. It was just her luck to get her hopes up for nothing.

50: Now

Jani had forgotten about that legend. Reba Auntie had told it to her in passing, she was too old for that kids' stuff by the time she had arrived at Deer Commons. Jani wondered if she could have even enjoyed it as a kid, the Borderlands had forced her to mature too early. Vampire snakes would have been no match for her and Momma. When she first came to Deer Commons she cared so much. She held that with her still but somehow it faded, she had gotten used to a new pressure, different from the Borderlands.

She hadn't wanted the villagers of Deer Commons to pity her or to fear her. She tried to shed that skin, be more like them. And so, obsessed with proving her worth in Deer Commons and having no skill at leisure, Jani learned everything she could about the trees they had within their walls. Something she was curious about, those junky elm trees. The elms of Deer Commons grew quickly as young saplings but when they emerged towards maturity, the invasion *always* got them, the worst was when it quickly spread from one elm to the next. This was another reason The Council held their law, their practice. If one villager left and came back spreading word of the world, good or bad, it would cause unease, unrest. The Council didn't want to spread roots, communicate widely. The Council was happy there were rarely vagrants showing up at the gates.

Jani thought of the legend, how The Council didn't want the world to know Deer Commons existed. The Council had forgotten about the billboards, the advertisements directing travelers to them. When Jani arrived, she hadn't thought to mention them. On her way to Mirror Marsh, they were all covered entirely in green, no longer readable, *all day* was one phrase Jani had been able to make out. She remembered how she had sounded out the billboards the first time she saw them. How she had been scared and excited to be so close to a world that had once been part of Momma's.

Jani had thought the old metal billboards looked awful, frightening, decayed over the decades since the collapse. She remembered what Sofi hypothesized about the grove in Deer Commons, that if the elms were kept isolated from one another, a few may thrive. But even through the best quarantine Sofi and the other Arborists could set up, the disease would still somehow hop, most elms eventually succumbing to the rot. Not being able to pull nutrients up from the soil to feed led to a slow death, all hope of potential as a sapling lost on the journey to maturity.

Jani prayed the elms felt no pain.

51: When

"Water is the source of life or the source of death for all creatures. We can't live without it," Manasa said as the two women sat on the top steps of the stepwell, their toes barely skimming the water. Prem had thought of her therapist's advice, feeling a new sensation might help, sober Manasa up.

"Take it all and sell it," Manasa cackled.

52: When

"What better gift could I give to Mother Earth, to pay respect, than to build this stepwell to honor her? To have believed in the promise of pure, clean water to anyone who stops here, human or beast," Manasa's query to Prem was genuine.

Prem had no answer to give, she was stuck driving home from the stepwell in the dark. And she couldn't leave Manasa here in this condition, she'd have to walk her back to her cottage, with all the wilderness surrounding them in the dark.

53: Now

Jani stood holding one of Drishti's notebooks, flipping through it, seeing it had been discarded with mostly blank pages. Jani was sick to her stomach; Drishti never would have left this behind. Whoever had stolen and then discarded it didn't understand the notebook's value.

Her first few weeks in Deer Commons were full of joys that trigger Jani with sadness. If only Momma had made it with her. She had cried herself to sleep wishing Momma knew she had finally found safety. Discovering the children of Deer Commons had not yet exhausted their supply of pre-collapse notebooks and chalkboard tablets was difficult to comprehend. Jani's Momma was always on the search for replacements, and it was a real special treat when Momma would tear out a sheet of paper for her. And what Momma would have given for an erasable tablet they could have played with together, instead of drawing in the dirt with whatever they could. Jani had carried one stick for years, Momma teasing her about her writing wand. But Jani had created that utensil, gifting Momma one as well.

"A magic wand for you Momma," Jani had said.

Jani still kept a few of Momma's paper pages with her, hidden with her underthings, her most precious possessions as they were proof of her and Momma's love. Notes Momma had made and had no use for, the margins of the paper good enough to entertain Jani or Jani's favorite, little sketches Momma drew on Jani's practice pages, to make her smile; always telling her she was lucky Momma didn't give her grades.

The idea of competing in school frightened Jani. Momma had said what it was like for her when she had been young, she got in a lot of trouble during school hours, teachers never liked her, but she was really smart, she could pass the quizzes and exams without ever having done the homework. Jani knew she was a disappointment to Momma in this way, she could read but not very well. It wasn't her favorite, like counting, or learning about what was in front of her. Jani would never be over it, always conscious of how she was still slow as an adult, always trying to put reading off until she was alone, wondering what the other villagers said about their Commander who always made Hans take over when it came to presenting updates, solutions, strategies. Those long words always got her, she didn't mind answering questions but needing to read, in front of them all, it was agony.

Everyone in Deer Commons knew how to pronounce things correctly, Jani's slang often made them laugh at her, straight to her face and there was nothing she could do about it but laugh too, playing along. A Commander can't lose their temper unless the situation is appropriate for them to be losing their temper. She hoped stealing Hans' mannerism of silence had led her neighbors to think Jani was stoic, thoughtful, logical, careful. That they didn't speak about her after she walked by, holding her tray and finding a seat in the cafeteria, discussing her inadequacies, qualifications, and wondering where else she may be slow if she was a slow reader.

The Council had accepted her because she had powers, strengths that Deer Commons needed but Jani knew they respected her less for the powers she didn't share with them.

When Jani was young Momma had teased her over it, saying when she was in school, she was in the gold reading group but her daughter somehow ended up in the brown reading group. Jani knew her momma loved her so much and wouldn't ever be mean to her beloved daughter, but she cried silently that night learning she had disappointed her momma without even trying. Jani had wanted to be smart so bad; she knew how much Momma admired that. Those that were safest were the ones who held on to those traditions of learning, their kids were safe, taught at home, pooling their paychecks together to pay for a teacher to move in with them. In Deer Commons a school had already been set up, day care through extension learning, it had taken quite a while for schooling to change for the villagers where Momma had pulled Jani out of school as soon as she heard what was happening, single mothers being separated from their children. Deemed unfit for any reason. Momma would have chosen to die before becoming a worker wife.

For that reason she never told Momma the truth, knowing Momma wanted gold for her daughter. Jani lying when asked her favorite color, *Orange Momma! Purple Momma!* Never deciding on one, thinking Momma would think Jani's *real* favorite color was dumb and disappointing Momma even more.

Brown was everywhere, that didn't make it special to Momma. Special to Momma was rare. Gold was rare.

Jani saw abundance as special and she saw in brown abundance, digging her toes in the dirt when they made camp, making little rivers in the earth as she dragged her toes in towards her body, cleansing them with Mother Earth, making Momma so mad, telling Jani not to get dirty, but Jani knew that earthy, wet, brown smell, was clean. It was the same smell after the rain fell. Fresh and light. Oh, and chocolate brownies. Coffee. So many of Momma's favorite things from before were brown and she had to know it. Jani watched her Momma's face light up in delight whenever they'd find a treasure of brown items like those, Jani had laughed out loud under the beautiful brown oak tree, watching a momma bird feed her babies and thinking of the time they had found that roost of chickens and their eggs, all in beautiful shades of brown, some even sparkling like jewels it seemed to Jani.

Jani also remembered times of truly feeling worried for Momma, sorry for her momma, always searching for gold, for a notebook with all empty pages for Jani. For a bottle that was brand new, a pair of socks still in their plastic wrap, crisp and white, thinking it was sad that Momma couldn't see the beauty Jani saw, how Jani liked her bottle that was worn from her grip, how Momma had shared the socks and Jani hid her dislike, they had been so itchy and stiff.

The natural shades of softness surrounded them and Momma forgot they were there. That they were special. Jani had done the same when she had grown up. Maybe that was what happened when you walked into Deer Commons.

Decades later that one comment about being in the brown reading group had stunted Jani, the shame associated with brown cementing her perceived inadequacy, her lack of intellectualism in front of The Council, reminding her of her place in Deer Commons.

54: When

"How did you get permission to construct on this sacred land, especially so quickly?" Prem wanted to ask, "And who do you expect to visit? How do you expect people to get here? I noticed it seems like there's no intention of road placement to get to the stepwell. No signage showing it's nearby. How were those decisions made?"

If only Manasa wasn't dancing with herself, standing on the top step with the water washing her feet. The light of the full Blood Moon reflecting her dance in the pool.

As though she could hear Prem's thoughts Manasa gave her answers while laughing lightly, pulling her dupatta, heavy with mirrors and beadwork, around her shoulders as she spoke, "We won't always have fuel and electricity. There's no commitment to it I can see, what about you? A way for it to be available to all. So, who can come here? I wanted the common folk and clearly the universe has wanted to challenge me, see me get creative.

"But when it was needed, any and all would always be able to come here for clean water. Maybe travelers who need rest, if they arrive upon our creation, they feel comfortable and safe and welcome to take shelter here. But history has taught us that water is life and getting water is women's work. Women bring life, we try, don't we?" Manasa crowed.

"So, you've built a monument celebrating women from the past and from the future?" Prem suggested, unable to decipher Manasa's words.

"A remembrance of our shared suffering without water," Manasa fluttered her eyelashes as she took a step forward, "I'm ready for the demonstration."

55: When

"And how long did it take to build this?" Prem inquired, hoping Manasa would turn around, wishing she had some ego and interest in discussing the two storied stepwell itself.

"Oh, as long as you'd expect. Too long! What boring questions these are!" Manasa laughed, "Come on. You did your research. A private property paid for in full? The only other competing offer the opportunity to create a landfill? A buyer for that creepy snake filled marsh?" Manasa bent over in laughter, resting her red palms on her knees and Prem shot up, worried Manasa was going to fall over into the depths of the stepwell.

Manasa wiped the tears from her cheeks, "Who cares about a crazy snake lady? Several ecological groups spoke to what a good idea it was for overall health of our ecosystem. I had money for construction and permits and lawyers. I've learned, I've suffered, and I've completed my task."

Prem wanted to tug Manasa backwards, to get her out of the stepwell but was worried she'd look just as crazy as her, damaging their relationship.

"Ah yes, always delaying our return to nature," Manasa pondered as she swirled her big toe in the water, "You know something else we always say about snakes?"

Prem shook her head no, again hiding her unease. There was no one keeping her here, she could just leave. But she couldn't. If anything happened to Manasa after she left, Prem wouldn't be able to live with herself.

Manasa didn't wait for Prem to move, to say her goodbye. Slurring her speech Manasa shared her snake fact, "They can grow forever. There is no limit to their potential as long as they have enough nutrients. Isn't that nice?"

56: Now

Jani trudged through Mirror Marsh, careful not to get stuck in the muck. After bringing Drishti back to Deer Commons she'd need *two* baths. She stepped over puddles as she thought back to her first night at Reba Auntie's.

"Ten days is a long time to be in isolation beti," Reba Auntie had explained as she gestured to the strange tables in her living room. They were taller than dining tables, narrower too. Jani wondered about the absence of chairs.

"What's the padding for?" Jani had questioned the strange devices.

Reba Auntie smiled, "For our comfort. Lying on a massage table without padding would hurt!"

Reba Auntie patted on one of the massage tables, "You'll find a robe in the bathroom, slip in after your bath and we can meet back here. The workers will be here in two hours. Plenty of time."

Jani had followed Reba Auntie's instructions, thinking she was in a fairy tale. She returned to Reba Auntie's living room and thanked her, and Reba Auntie introduced Jani to Stacey and Basil, who were helping with their massages today.

Jani wondered what they must have thought, Jani embarrassed as she followed Reba Auntie's instructions and realized Reba Auntie had slipped in nude between the sheets on the tables, kept warm with hot stones. Jani was wearing a pair of loose cotton pants and a too large for her button-up shirt, clothes she had found in the closet of her designated bedroom.

She was so embarrassed. No one said a word about it, Stacey gave her a massage above her clothes. The buttons buried into her sternum as she laid on her belly, Jani clenched her eyes shut through the discomfort, wiggling her face through the strange O shaped pillow.

Jani heard Reba Auntie's promise of extra rations and days off in exchange for their discretion, apologizing for Jani, explaining what had happened, to extend kindness because it wasn't her fault.

Later Jani went to the library and looked up the word Reba Auntie had called her, if she was what they had worried about at the gate, and understood, it was true. Jani just couldn't help being a bit feral.

57: When

Prem stood on the step behind Manasa, not enjoying the water which lapped up to her shins, she hadn't planned on using the stepwell at all but wanted Manasa to consider her a good sport.

"Now the construction of the stepwell, we did do something witchy for that, didn't we? Something interesting for your story Prem," Manasa spoke with her eyes closed. Prem looked at the water, watching the light bounce against it, dancing as Manasa was.

Prem wondered if Manasa could handle herself, she wanted to ask but didn't want Manasa to feel any shame. Riley had talked about their case studies before, and even so Prem was so naïve that she hadn't picked up on Manasa's substance use. Her slurring of words, her drowsiness, her explanations for so much. It all made so much more sense. Prem was determined to help Manasa with her article, the community would pay for rehab, she was certain she could make a good spin from this. Heath could fundraise for the paper off that. Prem was glad Manasa's focus was on the water, she didn't want to be caught looking so excited while Manasa was so troubled.

58: Then

Ana was lost in the People Profile she was reading in the *Gazette*, an interview with a medical student who said that while abstinence had been the recommendation to avoid pregnancy for most of history, for most of history people wanted to plan their pregnancies and there was nothing unhealthy or perverted about using hormonal birth control options or intra-uterine devices to prevent pregnancy, along with condoms to prevent sexually transmitted infections. That while she wanted to be a psychiatrist not a gynecologist, she was aware some patients may lack information and not *know* about pregnancy planning, that withholding this information was a form of reproductive coercion, that unplanned pregnancies put both mother and baby at risk. That there was absolutely nothing wrong with wanting to prevent pregnancy, Ana looked up from the profile and smiled when she saw Raven approaching her desk. She was excited to discuss it with Raven, the doctor wanted to increase access to medical care for all and Raven had been looking for meaning from her legal work, had been discussing offering pay-what-you can and pro-bono work just like this doctor in the profile wanted to do one day.

She held out the paper to Raven, she'd want it back, above the People Profile the *Gazette* had another feature on Rufus, who had gained accolades from across the state when he protected a small boy who had gotten lost when on a walk with his parents. Ana didn't believe Rufus protected the young boy but had just recently had enough to eat so hadn't needed to kill the small human.

Ana was happy to have Raven visiting in the Executive Suite and left shocked by Raven ignoring her offering, the newspaper she was holding out.

"Hey Ana, do you have a minute to talk?" asked Raven.

"Sure, what's up?" Ana wondered if this had to do with the upcoming Halloween party, they were meeting tomorrow to confirm everything was set for Friday's costume party.

"Did you do the dishes in the staff breakroom?" Raven inquired quietly.

"Oh, yeah. I had time on Friday afternoon; Mr. Paisley had me make sure the fridge was stocked with inventory and the smell was just too much for me. I figured if there were that many dirty dishes, that meant there were too many dishes in the breakroom, so I packed some up. Do you want them back?" Ana worried Raven thought she had stolen the dishes.

"Ana, is it your job to do the dishes?"

"No, I don't think it's anyone's job, right? I don't mind helping…"

"Yeah, but who asked you to help?"

Ana had nothing to say at that and fumbled, trying to come up with a reason for Raven for why she did the dishes. Raven held up her hand to let Ana know Raven did not want any excuses.

"You see Ana, Faith and I have refused to do the dishes for months. There's no service that comes into our breakroom to do the dishes, they just would magically get done one day, by one of us, and then the next day the sink would be full again, the counters covered, you name it. Faith and I have been carrying our own dirty dishes home every day, avoiding using the breakroom and then you decide to help, when it's not even your breakroom! Don't you eat at home every day? Why did it bother you so much when you only have to spend a few minutes every other week in there?"

Ana felt awful, she thought Raven and Faith would have been pleased to see the tidied breakroom. She hadn't known they carried their dirty dishes home every day although she had picked up on their avoidance in using the breakroom.

"Raven, I'm really sorry," Ana apologized, "You are absolutely right. I thought I was helping you when you never even asked for my help. Do you think there's anything I could do now to make it up to you and Faith?"

At Ana's apology, Raven softened. She had walked up to the Executive Suite expecting a fight, Mr. Paisley's assistants usually thought they were above the members of the Sales Team, forgot that she was a lawyer not just the lady who did the work Willard didn't think needed doing, and Raven had made a mistake of her own assuming Ana was like every other one of Mr. Paisley's assistants, was like every one of her supervisees.

"I'm sorry too," Raven began gently, "I should have waited before racing upstairs when I saw the dishes had been done. I lost my temper and that was wrong of me. I had never told you not to do the dishes either, how could you have known? It's just so frustrating. I've talked to Mr. Paisley about it, and he told me to get my direct reports to do their own damn dishes. And they don't! I'm their boss, telling them what to do and they still won't do their own dishes, thinking they can leave them for the magical dishwasher who stops by the breakroom every once in a while. It is so frustrating how the men who work here never clean up their spills or do their own dishes, just make dirty ones."

Ana was about to say that she understood and everything was okay as far as she was concerned when they heard Wayne's cough. Raven and Ana hadn't noticed him waiting in the doorway to the Executive Suite.

"It's kinda sexist of you to say the men never do the dishes Raven," Wayne admonished while waving his coffee mug at them, "Did you wash this one Ana?"

Ana looked down at the local section of the *Gazette*, wishing she could live in the wild with Rufus as she shook her head no.

"Ha!" Wayne exclaimed, "Don't worry Ana, you did nothing wrong. Raven may be a manager but she's not your boss, and she's not mine. Willard is and let's see what he has to say about Raven's sexism."

Ana shrugged apologetically at Raven as Wayne settled into the couch in the reception area.

"Thanks for your time Ana," Raven assured before she turned and left, completely ignoring Wayne and everything he had said.

"God, she's such a bitch!" Wayne baited after a few moments.

"I'm sure she was just checking on me," Ana answered, not wanting Raven to get into any trouble all because Ana couldn't stand a dirty breakroom she didn't even use.

"Don't be so naïve Ana," Wayne belittled condescendingly, "That's how these feminists get you, their propaganda. And don't let her get under your skin! You were right to do the dishes!"

Mr. Paisley opened the door to his office and Wayne stood up.

"Yo Willard! Can Ana make me a cheese and fruit plate? I'm starving!"

"Sure thing Baby Eddie," Mr. Paisley smiled at Ana, "Don't think we want coffee, get us two of those sparkling cinnamon waters too Ana! And don't forget my straw!"

"Sure thing!" Ana replied to no one as she looked at the *Gazette* on her desk. The two brothers had already stepped into the private office and closed the door, not expecting a response.

59: When

Prem wondered if it was unhygienic to drink the same water you walked into, the same water those beasts of the marsh Manasa mentioned drank from and at that thought decided she'd prefer the more hygienic option, even if it was in one of those evil plastic bottles Manasa had gone on about. She couldn't be expected to always remember to bring a thermos with her, especially with more and more public water fountains being removed due to the rising costs of maintaining them. When you're out and about, it's easiest to just buy a bottle of water; she didn't need anyone judging her, she judged herself most harshly of all. Maybe in a few years, after she had a regular column, a regular income, then she'd be the type of woman who had her life together but for now, she was struggling.

60: When

"I sought a water diviner, after I selected Mirror Marsh. I saved for so long, this was all I ever wanted. My legacy. I want no children. I want no skyscrapers named after me. No charities. Something that can actually be a benefit to all," Manasa rambled quietly. After a pause again Manasa softly spoke, "There are so many ecosystems here, we aren't far from oak savannahs or swamps, are we? Divination confirmed what I knew about this location. I learned however I could. I didn't attend university but that didn't mean researchers didn't help me understand. I wrote them, and they helped me. We did all want the same thing. A healthy Earth.

"I felt there was water running underground and they heard it. With their guidance we knew exactly how deep we would need to dig in order to create this water source for all creatures, one which would be here for them always.

"On a day I knew Manasa Devi would be happy to learn of our work, I held a ceremony. With the water diviner and several of my friends who were helping to dig and build and learn. Donating their experience, their labor, and their energy. We gave thanks to Mother Earth for providing. We began to dig and placed offerings, sweets and treasures of ours presented in a copper pot," Manasa pointed, "Yes, just like those, pots for anyone who needs water, available for their use. We saved one to gift to who my parents had prayed to, Manasa Devi, to protect us from snakebites and disease and so that the marsh would prosper for all creatures who live here. We hoped to please and honor her. Our markings and offerings, are buried under the water, buried underneath the stone. We left them for Manasa Devi's blessings. I prayed she would guide me to continue doing what was right."

61: Now

Jani found Reba Auntie looking out for her, she could have ended up in the dorms with the workers, but Reba Auntie had extended kindness to her. No one else had offered their home. Living in the luxury behind the gate was what Momma had always wanted for her. Within a day Jani went from eating grass to using cloth napkins as she sat in quarantine, folded underneath the plate on her stainless-steel tray, steam rising from the meal.

A few days after the incident with the massage, Reba Auntie felt confident that Jani was ready for a test, that it was time for Jani to mingle, and so, the two went to the club house for their meal. Reba Auntie separated from her suddenly, they had stood in line together, assembling their stainless-steel trays and then Reba Auntie surprised Jani by wandering off, calling to Jani as she steered her way to her own table, telling her that she was going to sit with some friends and she'd find Jani when she was done with her meal. Jani stood standing at the end of the buffet where all the cutlery and napkins lay, trying to figure out where she should sit, wondering if she missed instructions from Reba Auntie. Was she supposed to invite Reba Auntie to sit with her? Her momma had been so worried about this, all the manners Jani wouldn't know from living without others. She watched as most of the people her age came in the line, they all knew one another, laughing and scooping onto each other's trays. Jani was pushed to the side as several of her younger neighbors jostled past her, shoving her as they hurried to their seats with their overflowing trays. Jani had stood worried she should go back and pile her plate, take as much as she could that the people of Deer Commons were offering because they would be kicking her out soon.

She didn't notice Jeff Uncle stand from his table until he was approaching her, she began to move aside, assuming he needed something behind Jani.

"Jani, I'm Jeff. I'm sure you've heard nothing about me."

Jeff invited her to sit with him and his wife, Lara, they had been seated at a table for four. She sat across from them; Jeff had moved a bouquet of wildflowers from the center so that he could see her clearly when they spoke. They didn't ask her anything, let her sit and eat and learn about Deer Commons. On the walk back home Reba Auntie walked ahead with Lara Auntie and Jeff Uncle walked beside Jani. He told her that Myles had mentioned he had known Jani's mom.

Jani made no change in expression, just kept walking until they got back to Reba Auntie's. Reba Auntie thanked them for inviting Jani to dine with them and corrected Jani when she gave her goodbye.

"Thank you, Lara Auntie and Jeff Uncle," Jani repeated after Reba Auntie.

Lara Auntie and Jeff Uncle waved before walking back to their home. Jani still held her expression, frozen, unsure of Jeff's motives. Of how much Reba Auntie might know.

"Jani?"

Jani froze at the sound of Jeff Uncle's voice in Mirror Marsh.

62: When

The billboards had been everywhere, there'd likely be ads in the same issue that ran her story on Mirror Marsh. Prem felt sick as she anticipated where she had to take the interview, not wanting to interrupt Manasa describe the ceremony but being realistic about how under the influence and sleepy Manasa had become. At any point Manasa could fall asleep, change her mind and end the interview.

"As you see, we've left spots for lanterns," Manasa turned her head to show Prem and then began to walk back up the steps, "Any visitor with oil will be able to use these light sources. I wish for eternity. The same type we used to honor Manasa Devi have been adhered to the structure, to keep away all *evil* spirits who would try to haunt our sacred water space. The giving of water to all who need it is the greatest gift and there are many who despise charitable acts such as these.

"There are some who believe they are in charge of determining who is deserving of water. Wanting to control Mother Earth. Those that seek power over nature, who else may they seek power over Prem?"

Prem didn't want to answer, despite the darkness she could see Manasa's lips were trembling and that made her own eyes were fill with tears. At first Prem had wanted Manasa to like her, for them to end this interview as friends, with promises to keep in touch, and instead she wanted to return to her familiar uncomfortable feelings, wishing that the only thing on her mind was the steep climb up Hell's Hill in the dark.

"May the divine Mother protect those seen as resources to be sold instead of valued as precious life," Manasa spoke to the water.

63: Then

"Did anything happen?" Ana probed after she joined Faith and Raven at the conference table. She knew something had to have happened when Wayne met with his older brother. Raven hadn't been scheduled to meet with Mr. Paisley and he had requested Ana pencil Raven in at the last minute, something he never wanted to do. The meeting had ended quickly, and Raven had left the suite without even acknowledging Ana.

"Don't worry about it," Raven counseled, not looking up from her salad.

"Is this about the dishes?" Faith asked.

Ana looked at Raven. She had thought about her part in causing problems for Raven and had decided she wouldn't act or speak on Raven's behalf. Especially after what she heard Mr. Paisley tell Wayne. Ana had had difficulty sleeping the past two nights. Raven had been so welcoming towards her, more than any other employee, including Wayne who she had been spending almost all her time with on the weekend. Ana wanted to be sure not to make the same mistake twice, she wouldn't act because *she* was uncomfortable. Ana had thought about her own upbringing and what Ammi had taught her about what it meant to be dirty. What it meant to be clean. And who was responsible for that. From now on, she wouldn't act by making excuses, saying no one else could do it, that no one else knew how to do it. She'd decided she would *ask* where she could help when she felt she needed to do something, needed to take action and that if she didn't, she would *own* her actions. Tell the truth, she had cleaned the staff breakroom for herself, not for anyone else.

Raven ignored Faith and kept all conversation to what was written on the agenda which was all about what was needed to be ready for the Halloween Party. Ana took part while admiring Raven. It had been so brave of her to bring her issue to Ana, to trust that Ana could take the scolding, that Ana could hold Raven's upset. Ana could imagine how difficult it must be for Raven, Mr. Paisley consistently referred to her team as the WWW sales*men* even though Raven was the driving factor behind their sales and success. Behind *Willard's* success. Ana wondered if Raven ever got lost how Ana had been, lost thinking about how an expectation of 'clean up after yourself' was interpreted as misandry by the Paisley brothers.

64: When

Heath had wanted an underdog's story and Prem considered how she was an underdog too, gathering the courage to speak while she knew Manasa was hurting.

"Manasa, should we discuss the ruling on the Marigold River? It's impact on the Mirror Marsh Stepwell?" Prem gently requested, her face showing her sweetest, most fake smile as her heart raced.

Manasa's face hardened; her demeanor seemed to darken the space where they stood.

"Manasa?"

Manasa had turned away from Prem, asking, "Would you be a dear and get me two?"

Prem turned and followed Manasa's gaze to the line of copper pots lined against a wall of the stepwell. She tried to grab Manasa's eye, but it appeared she was lost in her own world.

"Sure, for the demonstration?" Manasa ignored Prem's question but still Prem half jogged past her tote bag and sandals to the wall to gather two of the copper pots. Prem hastily walked back and called to Manasa, telling her, "I should probably leave after this, it's getting late."

Manasa said nothing as she tied her dupatta as though she was a beauty queen wearing a sash, Prem handing Manasa the copper pots but she only took one, tying it to the longer end of her dupatta, and then reaching towards Prem for her second vessel.

"Here, let me help you," Prem moved to grab the pot from Manasa when she saw she was struggling to hold and continue standing in the water, "I can receive the benefit of the demonstration with just one pot, no need to struggle."

Manasa slapped her hand away and Prem gasped, tripping backwards up the steps, landing on her bottom.

Manasa did not acknowledge Prem's fall and took a step forward. Down.

Prem stifled a scream; she had pushed away from the stone step to stand up and saw a tiny snake swim out of the water and slither away from her on the step. Prem steadied herself, remembering Manasa's comment, a brain was always looking out for snakes.

Prem thought Manasa hadn't noticed her restrain her fear of snakes but was wrong.

"Some are so quick to kill them," Manasa continued to descend, "Fearing what they don't know. Destroy their habitat, what does it matter? Snakes are different so we should get rid of them, those idiots think. Who cares about this wildlife?" Manasa almost tumbled as she stopped to place the copper pot inside her dupatta, swaddling it as though it was a baby.

"They don't worry about other people, why would they worry about what happens with no water for these animals to drink, with no snake populations to survive. How can they profit off a stupid snake? Why worry how so many rodents would spread disease then? Without our dear friends keeping their numbers down? And the pain and sadness of how these animals die. This Earth is our home and provides for us and that isn't good enough," Manasa mourned.

"So, you'll fight it? You'll fight Paisley?" Prem walked forward, hoping to catch up to Manasa when she saw two more snakes rush past her onto the heat retained in the stone stepwell, stopping her in her tracks.

Manasa laughed again, agreeing, "I don't need to fight Paisley or his family from cutting the river off from feeding the stepwell and Mirror Marsh. I have lived with nature and have learned her patience."

"Paisley's Places. Deer Commons? You're not going to do anything?"

"I didn't say that; I said I'd be patient," Manasa said as she took another step.

65: Now

Jani was convinced she was staring at a ghost. There was no way Jeff Uncle could have survived. An original landowner from Deer Commons surviving on their own in the Borderlands was impossible.

The two stood staring at each other. Jani had never seen Jeff Uncle in such a state. She had forgotten what it was like, how she had gotten so used to just suffering through scrapes, bug bites, thirst, and tears and holes in everything she wore. Just as under the oak without the scent of cinnamon, she no longer noticed how there were fewer insects in Deer Commons than her days and nights in the Borderlands. How they had a never-ending source of clean water somehow. How the Couturiers welcomed dropping off clothes to be mended and offered new clothes created from scraps. Jani thought back to discovering the agility course for pets and children to play in. Once, when much younger, Jani had been chased by a pack of wild hounds, Momma doing what she sometimes had to do. Jani remembered their yelps and had heard the same sounds coming from the agility course, their masters correcting them by tugging their leashes, a loud, sharp voice teaching the pups their errors. Jani hated that some villagers called themselves anyone's master but in Deer Commons they bred very cultured breeds of canine for their very cultured residents, per Anderson, their Livestock Liaison. Jani was close with Anderson and his wife Nell, who also worked with the animals of Deer Commons. As Commander, she knew her neighbors well and that included their roommates, however many legs they may have. Jani liked the dogs in Deer Commons a whole lot more than the ones in the Borderlands.

It had been so strange and wonderful, like so much of life in Deer Commons. Jani thought it was fun having animals she knew that were her friends, magical almost that she could say hello to one and they'd come running, join her wherever she was seated outside. Corgis, border collies, and of course, all of Saaya's Pride. Those little kitties, many of whom were black furred with extra toes always made Jani's day. And they worked much harder than the canines, keeping all rodents out of the mess hall, dining facilities, and kitchen pantries. Looking at Jeff Uncle reminded Jani of Drishti's empty notebook. How even the residents that were afraid of the black kitties were worried along with the rest of the village about them, concerned the snakes may overtake and consume their beloved animal friends.

"C'mon," Jeff Uncle said as he gestured for Jani to follow him, "Drishti will be glad to see you."

Jani's face burned with shame. Had Jeff Uncle told Drishti what Jani had been commanded to do to him?

"You hungry?" Jeff Uncle twittered, calling back through the marsh.

66: When

"Manasa, would you let me join the demonstration?" Prem pleaded, "I can catch up."

Manasa shook her head no, "Let me demonstrate. You will have plenty of time to practice gathering water, Mirror Marsh belongs to you too Prem."

67: Then

"Holy shit!" Ana cried out from underneath the oak tree.

Wayne laughed and snuggled in closer to her, "Is that the first time you've heard them?"

"Oh my!" Ana laughed, "That was incredible! I wish I could talk back!"

As if the cranes heard her, one put out its call, the sound as loud as a horn, and Ana and Wayne dissolved into a fit of laughter.

"Oh my god, I'm laughing so much it hurts!" Ana spoke in between gasps, rolling on the flannel blanket they had laid underneath the oak.

Wayne pulled her closer and they kissed. When he released Ana from his grasp, she rolled on to her back and let out a sigh of contentment. Wayne coiled his fingers with Ana's, and they laid in the sun, the weather unexpectedly warm for the first day of November.

"How much longer until you own this place? Put down your landfill?" Ana asked, hoping the crane sighting might make Wayne realize the true value of this land. How it had to be more than a place to lay down the waste produced by human consumption.

"A few years at least, no one better buy it before me otherwise I won't be able to host the crane hunt before they build out the landfill. Don't steal my idea, Ana!" Wayne tickled Ana until she kicked him away.

"Please don't do that, I don't like it."

"Please don't do that, I don't like it," Wayne mocked, imitating Ana's voice. She hated when he acted this way; he only stopped when she withdrew, became so quiet that her unease was no longer entertaining for him.

"So, who do *you* think should have won the costume contest?" Wayne jabbered, before lighting a cigarette, whether to fill the silence or mock Ana further she was not sure.

Ana propped herself up on her elbows before fanning away his smoke, "What do you mean?"

"Well, it was kind of bullshit that you won."

"Why would my winning be bullshit?"

"You didn't even come up with the idea! The party planning committee suggested witches!"

"Okay, but I was the *best* witch. I put a lot of time into my costume, everyone else has too much of a life I guess," Ana retorted with an edge in her voice. Faith and Raven had dressed up too, in all black, with similar enough pointy hats to indicate their witchyness. Raven had come to work wearing all black, threw on the hat for the party, and then wore it out to her car as soon as the workday ended so she could go trick-or-treating with her kids. She had been pissed she had to miss her kids' Halloween Day Parade. Faith had hung around to help clean up after everyone left and had caught Wayne cornering Ana in the breakroom, trying to get her to ditch helping Faith to go with him and 'the boys' to Kilmer's.

"I mean, you have to agree it was sexist," Wayne complained petulantly.

"How was it sexist?!" Ana asked incredulously.

"Don't be so dumb Ana, no man is going to dress up as a witch."

"You could have dressed up as a wizard, which was printed on ALL the flyers. *Witch or wizard costumes recommended*?"

"Whatever, you only won because of the snake, using it as your wand. That was weird, and you had to explain to Willard how it even made sense!"

"Hey, don't get mad at me because your brother asked me about my name! You're the one who told him, and I didn't say you could!" Ana was livid that Wayne was mad at *her*, "Y'know maybe you would have won if you ever came to any of the Party Planning meetings."

"Yeah right, like Willard really wants me wasting my time there."

"But it is okay to waste Raven's time planning parties? She's a fucking lawyer and a manager! What do you even do?"

"God, why are you so obsessed with her? Do you want to be her or be WITH her?" Wayne stood above Ana and nudged her with his toe to get off the blanket.

"Wayne, do you really care *that* much about winning the contest? The prize was for everyone to share, Paisley's buying us *all* lunch."

"So, you admit my costume was better," Wayne towered above Ana.

"No, I'm saying my costume fit the theme AND wasn't a stereotype."

"Oh my God Ana!" Wayne yelled as he tried pulling the flannel blanket out from underneath Ana.

Ana stood to allow Wayne his tantrum, "All I'm saying is that there were a million costumes to choose from that didn't make a costume out of an ethnicity. That hurts people."

"Do you hear yourself Ana? You sound like those crazies that want to change mascots and shit. No one cares."

"You aren't listening! You *should* care!"

"FUCK IT!" Wayne shouted and threw the butt of his cigarette at the oak before storming off, his family's flannel blanket trailing behind him.

Ana crawled over to the cigarette butt and picked it up once she was sure it was out. She shoved it into the pocket of her jeans and then kneeled on the earth underneath the young oak and counted to ten. After that she gathered the belongings they had brought and tried carrying them through the meadow to where Wayne had parked. As she hurried towards his car she worried he would leave without her, stranding her there with all their things. She'd have to walk for a very long time to even find a phone to call for help. She got lost in her thoughts, figuring out a plan so she was prepared if she found out Wayne had left without her. Ana heard the sound of water moving and realized that she was lost. She stood in the meadow and turned in a circle, everything seemed to look the same, whatever direction she looked. She looked in the distance and saw the steep hill she'd have to climb if Wayne had left without her.

She began walking towards the hill, the guarantee she was directing herself towards Wayne's car and soon realized she had made her way back towards back to the oak tree, disoriented once again. Ana looked around and remembered her path, circling back the way she had just come. The days were much shorter now and once the sun set, the unseasonable warmness of this November day would be gone and Wayne hadn't even left her the blanket. She was tiring of carrying all of their things and realized she would have to leave them at the base of the hill if Wayne had ditched her, it wouldn't be possible to traverse up that hill in the dark safely, especially if she was carrying all of their trash.

Ana stopped in her tracks when she heard rustling in the grasses in front of her.

"Wayne?" she whispered.

There was no answer offered in return and the grasses had stopped moving. Ana took a deep breath and then started walking forward, she had to keep moving just as the sun was. She had only taken a few steps when she noticed green glowing eyes just a few feet in front of her. Ana froze, unsure of what to do, a feeling in her stomach telling her she was looking into her *own* eyes.

"Jesus Christ Ana! Hurry the fuck up!" Wayne shouted as he stomped through the grasses, waving his cigarette in anger.

Ana watched the large green eyes blink slowly, grow slightly smaller in retreat, and then blink at Ana once again. Ana wanted so badly to follow the melanistic bobcat as he pounced away, towards the bubbling sounds of the Marigold River.

68: When

Manasa selected her words as carefully as she navigated the steps which bound her to the water, balancing the copper pots on her hip and waist, "What helps Mirror Marsh? Keeps those at home here safe? Make sure these snakes survive. Work with scientists who care about the animals just as much as they care about using them to create anti-venom. Remember they warn us well first." Manasa stopped on the steps, the water up to her knees, completely soaking the petticoat and skirt she had worn.

Prem nodded, prodding Manasa to continue. Once Manasa had given her demonstration, dipped either copper pot into the depth of the stepwell, Prem would thank her and escort her back to her cottage, leave, find the truck, race home to write this article, to submit it to Heath. It would be over real soon.

Manasa stood still, the light from the moon reflecting off her dupatta's beadwork and mirrors, the edge of the copper pot.

With trepidation Prem stepped forward, stating, "Let me help you."

Prem watched the lights bounce across the water as Manasa moved forward and down. Prem felt herself stepping backwards, watching a much larger snake moving underneath the surface of the water in front of her. As she turned, she tripped and crawled forward on the steps, water splashing, thinking only of running away.

"Be patient," Manasa sung under her breath, "It is the way."

69: Now

Drishti had been delighted to see Jani, hugging her tight when she walked into Jeff Uncle's cabin. Jani had handed her the notebook she had found, and Drishti hugged her again, then led her to Jeff's kitchen table.

"It's small but nice," Jeff Uncle grinned to Jani after Drishti had left them alone, stepping outside to cook their dinner.

Jani saw the photographs spread across the table, the tissue they had been wrapped in carefully folded like Grover would have done, the stack of notebooks and papers, and Jani was surprised to see copies of newsprint, not the newspapers themselves. The Council had been right, Drishti had stolen from the Scriptorium. Jani was torn between looking at the stack of information, wanting to read, not caring that Jeff Uncle and Drishti may see her sounding out the old timey words and wanting to talk to Jeff Uncle, ask him what he knew about Mirror Marsh, the cultists that lived here that hated her neighbors, the serpents, if he had been poisoned by their skin, if he knew anything helpful from the beforetimes. She wanted to ask Jeff Uncle what Myles would have done if he was Jani. Momma had told her about all of the conflict between the different classes that led to the collapse. To be rich was all any human aimed to be, Jani was sure of it. The richest had seen no beauty in Mother Earth, they had seen just what they could take before they died. Take, take, take, hoard, hoard, hoard. If you weren't rich, you could act rich.

"Drishti enjoys cooking," Jeff Uncle commented, watching Jani look at the stack of newspapers Drishti had brought to Mirror Marsh, "She doesn't get to too often."

"She doesn't need to. She had more important work in the Scriptorium. Drishti should understand that she is not a cook," Jani commented, wondering if Drishti knew how to start a fire, safely. The simple life of Deer Commons stood out to Jani once again, in case she had almost forgotten how much harder staying alive was outside of the safety of her village. It reminded her of her youth in the Borderlands between all the claimed terrortories. If the wrong people saw smoke….

Jani knew it was time. "I'm sorry Jeff Uncle," she began.

Jeff Uncle shook his head, "I won't have any of that. We all do what we need to do to survive."

Jani had messed up her manners again, Jeff Uncle was referring to the last time she saw him where she was trying to remind him that she couldn't escort him back to Deer Commons. "We can stay for dinner," Jani lied, "but I've got orders to bring Drishti back."

"Why would I go back to Deer Commons?" Drishti argued.

70: When

Prem scrambled, pushing against the wet stone to find another path to Manasa.

Prem yelped as her sit bones smacked her hard stone, more snakes, they could have been the same ones or maybe it was a sign of how many there were. Manasa had promised that they didn't want to harm humans, that Prem would simply just have to move around them.

The water was nearing Manasa's waist, she stood in place and turned to Prem, the moonlight illuminated her form, looking to Prem as though Manasa was a deity, a giver of magic if not life.

"They want to leave you alone and to be left alone. Yet more fear those little snakes than the ones who seek cruelty as law," Manasa foretold.

71: Then

Mr. Paisley stood next to Ana as the staff of WWW filed in to grab slices of pizza and mingle while holding their greasy paper plates and plastic cups filled with bubbling energy drinks, courtesy of WWW and Mr. Paisley himself. Ana had arranged everything so that people could file in and make their plates and then efficiently transition to socializing once they had their food and drinks. As she watched Mr. Paisley greet his employees and accept their gratitude, she realized Mr. Paisley would still take credit if she had just stacked the pizza boxes on top of one another and left out a few rolls of paper towels.

"Hey Ana!" Faith chatted once the line to greet Mr. Paisley thinned out.

"Hey Faith!"

"Nice job on your costume and the party! Come join us!" Faith said, pointing to Raven leaning against the wall holding a plastic cup.

Ana looked at Mr. Paisley and he smiled down, dismissing her, "Yes, Ana, great job." Relieved to be excused from her hostess duties, she joined Faith and the two women walked over to the pizza boxes where Ana grabbed the remaining slice of cheese and balanced her plate with her stainless-steel bottle, which she had filled with water after she had finished her morning chai.

"Hey Raven, what's new?" Ana asked before taking a small bite of the tip of the triangle.

"Hey Ana. I'm not sure if Paisley told you, Gabby from accounting is returning on Monday."

"Gabby?" Ana asked as she covered her mouth.

"Yeah! You're going to love her Ana," Faith bubbled before letting out a burp, "Oops, sorry, too much of our Sparkling Wellness Waters!"

The room began to clear out while Faith and Raven caught Ana up on Gabby's situation. She had given birth to a healthy baby girl over two months ago but her boss Basel hadn't been particularly keen on her returning to WWW, he preferred to hire someone else, who wouldn't take the time off a new mom would need. No one had had time to post or interview for Gabby's position and Mr. Paisley had requested Basel call Gabby back for all of the end-of-year accounting reports that were due soon. Their sales had really taken off and Basel couldn't refuse Mr. Paisley's logic, it would be quickest to get Gabby back to speed and that way they could take their time hiring her replacement, if needed, after the new year.

Faith and Raven surprised Ana by never mentioning Gabby before. Maybe Gabby hadn't been on the Party Planning Committee. Ana had noticed the empty cubicle outside Basel's office but hadn't realized he was anyone's supervisor. Like the sales reps, it was often difficult to find Basel, he came and went when he pleased so Ana hadn't thought much about him at all.

"Who is taking care of their baby?" Ana asked.

"Gabby's in-laws are moving in with her and her husband. He's an ER doc so is home most weekdays but still needs his sleep."

"Wow, that's so much work."

"Yeah, Basel wasn't too happy about that. Thought it was selfish she was looking for more money," Faith rolled her eyes.

Raven shot her a look and Faith realized her mistake, widening her eyes and searching around to see if anyone overheard. Ana mirrored Faith's behavior and saw there were just a few sales reps left in the conference room, all huddled near the pizza boxes and soda bottles.

"Time to clean up!" Faith announced walking away.

Ana looked at Raven who smiled and nodded before walking away. Ana watched as Raven threw her plate into the trash before stopping to call out to Ana before exiting the conference room, "Excellent work Ana, thanks for throwing this pizza party together!" The sales reps noticed their boss leaving and as they hurried after her they shouted thanks at Ana while taking their plates and cups with them.

"Think there's room in the fridge?" Faith asked as she flopped open one of the pizza boxes, "This is a lot of leftover pizza."

Ana sighed knowing even if the pizzas were veg, she wouldn't eat *any* leftovers out of that fridge, "I guess I gotta go in there and at least look."

72: Now

Jani, Jeff Uncle, and Drishti found themselves around Drishti's cooking fire eating their vegetable stew. Jani wondered if the others had realized the three of them had never eaten a meal together while they were in the village. Before they sat on the logs Jeff Uncle had arranged for seating, they had taken a tour around the outside of his cabin. After they began eating Jani lost Hans' superpower, and no longer being able to stand the uncomfortable silence commented that she was impressed with all that Jeff Uncle had done, complimenting the kitchen garden Jeff had been able to put together without any seed provided by Deer Commons.

Jani realized her mistake, letting slip that she knew something had happened to the sack full of provisions The Council had given him in front of Drishti, outing Jeff's exile, if not his death. Drishti had shown no surprise, and this upset Jani. Jeff had lied, he had promised her that he hadn't spoken a word about Jani's visit to Drishti. As Jani was yelling Jeff was begging her to stop, to calm down, swearing that he hadn't told Drishti anything. Eventually they noticed Drishti's silence, her refusal to argue with them.

"Jeff didn't have to tell me anything," Drishti explained to Jani, "I read the records of every exile when I was doing my research in the Scriptorium. I know what the Commander of the Guardians must do. Why we're taught so young to never joke about wanting to go shopping outside of Deer Commons. To complain of the boredom of walking the same trails over and over again.

"I'm just so glad you didn't hurt him Jani," Drishti voiced.

Jani looked away from them, she didn't want her neighbors to see her shame.

"What did you do with the sack?" Jeff Uncle wondered.

"I handed it to The Council. Proof of your death. Just like I said. Why?" Jani spoke with venom, ashamed of her actions, embarrassed at what she had become. Momma had said to always protect the innocents and Jani had not been one in such a long time.

"I'll tell you after we clean up," Jeff yakked, ignoring Jani's tone.

Jani's betrayal still clung to her although Drishti and Jeff tried to strike it away.

73: When

Manasa walked forward slowly, Prem watching the water rising exponentially, it now reached Manasa's collar bones.
Prem overcame her fear, storming down the steps.

74: Now

Jani offered to dry the dishes when Drishti began washing.

"I'll help in a sec, I'm gonna find something. It's around here somewhere," Jeff Uncle quipped.

Drishti and Jani worked in tandem as Jeff Uncle tore through the few belongings in his cabin. He snapped his fingers and then pointed at the ceiling before diving onto the bed in the corner of the room. Jani and Drishti dried off their hands as they watched Jeff Uncle fling his clothes and bedding until he found a square pillow.

The three sat at the table as Jeff Uncle used a pair of scissors to gently cut the first few stitches of the pillowcase, before gently removing the thread. He pulled the stuffing out and then showed Jani and Drishti the pillowcase.

"See? See?" Jeff Uncle showed off.

"Did you make that pillow? It's lovely," Drishti politely said as she shifted to take a better look.

Jani didn't have Drishti's manners and grabbed the pillowcase from Jeff Uncle's hands, turning it inside out. "This one of our jackets?" Jani accused.

"Indeed," Jeff affirmed, pleased with himself.

Jani remembered that night. The ground had been as wet as it was in Mirror Marsh. There had been days of rain. Jani had felt pity for Jeff. She remembered thinking he was a fool for not taking one of his personal belongings, he had wind and waterproof jackets, technology from the beforetimes that helped your body heat stay in, vents that unzipped to let the heat of your body out. She had thought of his loss, that Jeff Uncle had left because he could no longer live without Lara Auntie. Her loss had been too much. She had thought maybe he had resigned to die after Lara Auntie had left their realm, that had explained away why he left his personal belongings to The Council to reassign after inventory.

"I suppose the Couturiers taught you how to sew?" Jani quipped as she showed Drishti the stitching.

"I learned *almost* on my own," Jeff Uncle smiled with pride, "Lara insisted on teaching me, she was so worried how I would survive without her."

"And no one noticed you kept the seeds from the plants in your kitchen garden."

"We had a good harvest that year," Jeff Uncle admitted, "The Council didn't ask for us villagers to chip in from our kitchen gardens for the seed library. There was enough to sow the following season. Drishti said that's not an issue now like it was sometimes. Now you don't have enough workers to harvest, huh?"

Jani fingered the pillowcase, noticing the gaps in between the canvas fabric and the nylon lining of Jeff Uncle's jacket as she admitted, "Things aren't good. The Council has gotten stricter. We've got curfews. It's for our safety. We have trouble seeing them during the day so at night… If you touch a snake you're quarantined. If bit…"

"If you get bit, they leave you on your own to get better," Drishti said angrily.

Jeff Uncle looked at each of his neighbors and then asked, "Why would they leave you and do nothing? The work still needs to get done."

"There's nothing *to* be done, there's no cure!" Jani spit with venom.

"That's true," Jeff Uncle rested his chin in his hand as he thought.

"That's why I'm here," Drishti blurted out, "There is a reason the serpents are coming after us. Why after all these years we're having problems."

Not wanting to hear Drishti's excuses for stealing Jani handed the pillowcase to Drishti, exposing the gaps, small pockets sewn between the two fabrics.

"I don't understand," Drishti said.

Jeff stood to address the first calls of the whistling kettle, "The Legend of Eadwayne. I knew it would be helpful to have seed to trade. I'm embarrassed to admit I didn't realize how helpful they'd be for me to survive."

75: When

Prem left Manasa on the stone, exhausted. She had done all she could, all she knew how to help. Prem scrambled to her feet and rushed into her sandals. She didn't know where Manasa's cottage was so would head towards Riley's truck.

She reached into her tote bag before she was plunged into the darkness of the meadow, alone with the Blood Moon. She made sure she had the keys to Riley's truck and then double checked the disposable camera. Twenty photos, twenty uses of the camera's flash to find her way to her parking spot, to find her way to get help.

76: Now

Jani hopped suddenly as she noticed a small snake slithering away from Jeff Uncle's garden, into the grasses of the meadow. She was waiting for Drishti and Jeff, they had both insisted on escorting Jani to the stepwell, to prove to her there was nothing that could be done. Drishti had tried her best to explain but Jani insisted on seeing with her own eyes. Drishti had let her hold the papers, copies she had made of ancient advertisements, Jani not believing they were real.

"I can't believe you don't trust me!" Drishti frowned.

Jani scoffed, "Trust? You ran away! Stole from the Scriptorium! The Guardians are on their own! The villagers are terrified and you aren't helping."

"All I've ever done is try to help! You are ignoring this Jani! They've been keeping secrets from *you*," Drishti shook the stack of papers at Jani, "The Council would have never granted us permission to investigate Mirror Marsh on our own if I came to you. To see if the snakes had been planted by cultists. Diplomacy, to even talk with others outside our walls is treason! I can't trust their version of stories. And frankly, neither should you! Look what they asked you to do to Jeff Uncle! Are you serious about trying to kill me?"

Jani burned as she hissed, "I would *never* do that to you. There's no way I can prove those papers are real. You could have had anyone in the Scriptorium fake those papers."

Drishti shook her head, "I didn't have any help. I learned on my own, the library had a book, taught me I could copy the newspaper if I had the right supplies. I traded in the kitchens for some wax paper and copied them by transferring the newspaper print to the wax paper and then from the wax paper to these paper pages when I got back home. Won't you at least look at them before you decide you won't believe me?"

Jani looked at where the snake had slithered to and thought about those advertisements, someone had paid a lot of money for such a small amount of text. The copies Drishti made were fascinating, Jani had no idea the Scriptorium kept such records. In between puppies and used kitchen appliances for sale and garage sale notices (reminding Jani of one of her earliest memories, collecting things for their new apartment, walking through strangers' garages and front lawns, garage saleing with Momma),

Drishti had circled the ones of note, explaining to Jani they had been called *Classified Ads*. Jani hoped she would be able to see them herself, there were a few for finding mates, she wondered what Hans would think when she quizzed him later. Jani had gotten distracted, trying to understand the language from decades past, asking Drishti, "What does 'SWF' mean?"

"You're missing the point," Drishti said, grabbing the papers back and then going through each one, "Here. *Join us Saturday! Stop the Marigold River Dam!* Here. *Earth Day is EVERY day, save Mirror Marsh! Join our letter-writing campaign!* And this one, *The stepwell is nearly empty, destroy the Marigold River Dam!*"

"What's this one?" Jani asked Drishti, *"Don't let Manasa's sacrifice be in vain, stop Paisley's Places!"*

Drishti explained as Jani read through them all, Drishti had them organized so they had gotten angrier, more desperate as Jani paged through. The ads surrounding these messages stayed the same, everyone in a normal routine, looking to get rid of or to find something while the ones Drishti had circled made Jani's heart fall. These people had been so desperate. Her momma had talked about them, their arrests. They had sounded crazy, had frantically tried to warn about the collapse, *RIP Rufus. Mirror Marsh is just the beginning. Fight for us, with us. Do not let the avarice of man kill our home. We have just one Mother Earth.* They had been right.

Drishti told Jani there were many more things in print about Mirror Marsh that she didn't copy. Letters to the newspaper they had printed from residents, worried about the wildlife at Mirror Marsh. Upset at the construction of Deer Commons.

"They said that if Deer Commons needed a dam to be built, they shouldn't build Deer Commons and people laughed at them," Drishti had said gently to Jani, "But the animals must be laughing now. Jeff showed me the stepwell, the water is near the top step, the ground water may keep rising."

"The Marigold River Dam is over fifty years old and hasn't been maintained for close to thirty. The snakes are just coming back to their home," Jeff Uncle agreed.

77: Then

Ana sat in her kitchen crying, a mug of chai cupped in her hands, wishing it had been handed to her by Ammi or Papa. Before she had left to go home for her lunch break, she had let Mr. Paisley know she wasn't feeling well and would be at home for the rest of the day. She knew she must have looked sick because she *felt* sick. Over twelve thousand were dead. Ana felt the burning behind her eyes. The report in that morning's *Gazette* said that summer's program resulted in over four thousand adults and nearly eight thousand juvenile or unborn rock rattlesnakes bountied. She had read a description of two brothers who hunted the banks of the Marigold River, searching for their dens and attacking to collect thirty eight rattlesnakes in one day, together nearly hitting the state record of collecting a twenty dollar bounty.

Mr. Paisley didn't seem to mind Ana leaving work early and she hadn't taken a single day off since she started working for him. Ana wondered if she could collect unemployment. Would the government know her parents' life insurance had paid out millions of dollars? That in just a few months she was set to collect revenue on the pharmaceutical discovered from their research on anti-venom? It was probably wrong of her to collect unemployment, but it felt wrong to touch their money. The money that had come from their work and their death. She had done not one thing to earn it.

The worst thing was that Ana had no one to talk to, to counsel her. She thought of Raven who had brought Gabby by her desk that morning to introduce the women to one another. Raven had a keen business sense and had seemed to trust or at least believe in Gabby. Ana decided she would call in tomorrow and return to her desk on Wednesday for Party Planning Committee. Mr. Paisley was ready to hear their plans for the Holiday Party and it would be a good excuse to talk to Raven alone in the conference room.

Wayne had a meeting with Mr. Paisley in the morning and Ana didn't care to see him and knew as long as she worked there, he would keep asking her to go to Kilmer's or worse, destroy what she had named for herself Mirror Marsh. Mr. Paisley had made it clear that part of her job included a special talent, the one which kept Wayne busy and happy, so he didn't annoy his big brother as much. So he didn't detract from the boss when the boys went out to Kilmer's on Fridays after work. So that Mr. Paisley didn't have to call a cab for him when he'd had too much to drink,

Ana was always there to do it. Wayne had never seen her kitchen table and grew more and more insistent, Ana always stopped at kissing, she allowed the groping but how long could this really go on? How much was this job worth?

Ana imagined pouring her problems out to her Ammi. What Papa would say if he saw her crying like this.

You're too good to work there.

Ana decided she would skip out on her receptionist duties tomorrow and spend the day looking into her balances and her parents' agreements and policies. And on Wednesday she'd ask Raven to help her figure out how much she'd have to save in order to go back to university on her own.

78: Now

Jeff Uncle, Drishti, and Jani traveled in single file on their way to the stepwell. Jani had been impressed by Jeff Uncle's machete; she had never seen him with a weapon before.

"I've only used it on grasses," he said when he saw the look on Jani's face, "I found a push mower, but it was covered in vines, I cut 'em out and it was all rusted up. So, we'll use the machete."

Jani hated being in the rear, she wouldn't have minded if it was Hans who was leading the way. She didn't trust that Jeff Uncle would be able to fight off any of the cultists who worshipped the Legend of Eadwayne.

"It's all a lie Jani," Drishti had said as they stood arguing, Jani insisting she be first so Jeff and Drishti could run back to the cabin if they needed to.

"There's no one living here besides me and all these furry and feathered creatures," Jeff Uncle lectured.

"And the ones with fangs and scales," Jani berated him as she pointed the problem out.

"And they don't attack without warning," Drishti finished the conversation leaving Jani standing behind until Jeff Uncle waved his machete for her to hurry up.

As they trudged through the meadow, three villagers of Deer Commons in a row, Jani thought of the summer Momma and her were joined by a boy a few years older than Jani, who had been a teenager. Jani hadn't trusted him at all, but Momma was in charge and Momma was sick of all the killing she'd had to do. The boy had begged for protection and Momma promised him that. Grover. Momma didn't believe his name was real, she had told Jani that. But Momma still invited him to travel and camp with them, leaving him with them when they were most vulnerable, Surya hidden for the night and only Chandra keeping watch, the moon's cool temper allowing so much to happen in the dead of night. So many predators excelled when Surya was resting, and Chandra was in charge. Momma promised she and Jani would keep watch, allowing Grover to sleep uninterrupted and that upset Jani too. *What was the point of inviting someone into their party if they couldn't pull their weight?*

As the weeks of spring turned into the longer days of summer, Jani slowly warmed up to Grover. Time breeds familiarity and Momma was the one who had taught her daughter about chosen family. How some people you'd never expect can become closer and take better care of you than your own blood. Jani didn't find Grover pathetic, he never tried to win her over. He could feel her keeping her distance, trying once or so a day to engage with Jani, until she wore down. And then so quickly, they became fast friends, Jani's first and only friend until Myles and Reba Auntie she considered. Remembering how Grover taught her many cool skills, starting with how to make insignificant items disappear.

Jani had watched him show off his magic skills for Momma for a bit. Seeking permission from both Jani and Momma first before folding the pages from an old phone book they had found and been carrying with them as fire starter for a very long time. At first Jani had said no but after seeing Momma say yes, she changed her mind the second night. She wanted Momma to be happy.

Grover tore two thin, faded pages, almost yellow in color but not quite, into roses and then handed one to daughter and mother. Jani stared in wonder at it, he had done it so quickly and yet it was so intricate. She wanted to unfold it to see how he had done it and also, keep it intact forever. She watched as Momma thanked Grover and handed it back to him. Grover smiled and then tossed it into the small fire pit they had dug, turning to Jani. Jani hadn't wanted to part with it and Grover asked if she wanted him to teach her the next time they camped, and she nodded, watching the flames.

"Keep it then, it may get squished in your pocket, but it'll be good for you to learn how to smooth out a page," Grover commented, providing the perfect excuse for Jani to hang on to his perfect creation for a few hours. She didn't bother hiding it, keeping it close to her head as she slept, pleasing Grover who hadn't known how to thank her, for letting her into their camp, sharing her Momma with him.

Grover and Jani grew closer and Momma began to relax a bit, watching the two play with paper airplanes, the first origami Grover taught to Jani. Occasionally worrying when they began to chuckle, Jani's Momma thinking the giggles may turn to guffaws and then into shouts, leading to the discovery of their camp. She wanted to shut it down, but she never did, her daughter had laughed so much when she was little, it seemed like every single time she saw her baby girl she was so happy and of course with the collapse, and then realizing Jani was approaching her own changes, Jani had grown so sullen and sad. And why wouldn't she be? What future had she left for her daughter? What future had *her* mother left for her daughter?

And so, Jani's Momma let the two continue to joke and have fun. She knew she wouldn't always be around and if Jani could protect Grover and Grover could protect Jani, there'd be two decent humans left in this realm to offer kindness and protection to other decent humans. She watched the shared humanity build between Grover and Jani and vowed to protect them.

One day the three of them were walking along the train tracks, Momma had wanted to show them some place important to her, a place that might have things they needed, Jani and Grover balancing on the rails across from one another, racing to see who was fastest when Momma called them back to her. She was crouching along the ground and pointed to the rocks in between the tracks, asking the two if they saw what she did. Jani noticed it first, Surya guiding her as a ray of light caused her to squint, reflecting off the shiny disc buried under some of the white and light beige rocks, those too marked by Surya, bleached by the sun.

Grover noticed where Jani's eyes had gone and almost shouted, then remembering that danger always existed around them. Why Jani's Momma had softly called them back, why they probably shouldn't have been racing ahead. Jani's Momma stood into her feet, out of her crouch, and held the disc between her fingers, passing it to Grover and then crouching down to dig one out for Jani.

Jani's cheeks felt hot with anger, she couldn't believe Momma had handed him the treasure first. She crouched down beside Momma, ready to dig into the rocks herself and her Momma snapped at her, quietly between clenched teeth, "Where are your gloves? Do you *want* to die?"

Jani stood up, hinging from her hips and stepped back from Momma in shame. It didn't seem Grover had noticed, he passed the disc over to Jani, explaining it looked like a penny from before the collapse. Jani of course had seen pennies before and angered at that. Forever relegated to being treated like she was a dumb kid. She looked at the disc as she held it in her palm, appreciating the dark honey brown color of the smooth and imperfect disc. Momma held her gloved hands out, displaying half a dozen discs, of various shapes, colors, and size. She threw them in her zip bag and then held out her palm, gesturing for Jani to hand the squished penny back to her. Jani did so, rolling her eyes to display her annoyance and then her Momma stuck the zip bag into her knapsack and the three continued on their way.

As they walked Momma told them both about the significance of the coins, how this was something kids used to do, for fun. Ride their bikes to train tracks and place coins on the tracks for trains to flatten, cheering as the trains rolled by, blasting their call, a horn with such dimension you heard it in your heart and belly. If on the ground you'd feel it in your sit bones, the train and horn shaking Mother Earth.

Grover couldn't believe parents would ever let their kids just do whatever like that, asking Momma how often they died. This caused Momma to lecture them both on staying connected to Mother Earth and when parents became more obsessed with their screens, their kids did too and then all the bad things happened. Everyone stayed inside, convinced the natural world was unsafe. Bugs and dirt and being itchy and hot, all the discomforts were just part of it. All the beings they passed felt those things too. It was okay to connect with our suffering and it helped us realize all of us want that same thing, to be loved and safe. It just wasn't always possible though, and that made them want it more.

Jani watched Jeff Uncle push through the cattails and grasses and steadied Drishti as she struggled to walk through the muddy Earth, thinking how that was how everyone she knew today had survived, by staying far away from the natural world.

79: When

Riley looked over to check on Prem. Prem stared out the window, wrapped in the itchy blanket the police had given her, tugging it tight across her body.

Riley was worried. The officer had offered no explanation. Prem had been driving erratically. Claimed she was hysterical when she had been pulled over. They would comb Mirror Marsh, they only had their flashlights in the dark and promised and update after daybreak, they'd use their canine officers, search Manasa's cottage.

Riley assured the officers she was an expert when they suggested holding Prem, checking on her mental wellness.

Riley didn't realize Prem had heard, instead was wondering what Prem must be thinking as she stared out the window.

Prem was thinking of the light from the officers' flashlights, bouncing about Mirror Marsh as she traced acorns, cat tails, snakes, and flowers onto Manasa's stainless-steel bottle, hidden to Riley and everyone else on Earth under her itchy blanket.

80: Now

Back then, that night as they camped, Jani watched as Momma handed her zip bag to Grover first. Before Jani knew it, she was steaming mad, angry tears in her eyes. Momma had shown it to *him* first. This time Grover noticing Jani's quiet anger, feeling uncomfortable with the attention he tried giving attention to Jani, who shoved the zip bag away from him in frustration, refusing, wanting him to feel stupid enough that he would go away, so it would just be her and Momma again.

Grover distracted himself from the tension by ignoring Jani's reaction, digging into the zip bag through the light discs. He took one of the honey-colored pennies out and did the trick for Momma, Jani looking at the ground between her feet as they sat together. Momma was genuinely impressed by Grover's magic trick, making the squished coin disappear and reappear, from within his palms.

Seeing pride on Momma's face, Jani grew even more outraged, distancing herself from them for the rest of the night. Momma asked him to repeat the trick and Jani stood up, claiming she was tired and began cleaning her things to lie down with her back them. She laid there and listened to them quietly discuss the coins and Grover's past with magic, his grandpaw had worked in a magic shop and passed his interest down to his son. Jani didn't care about Grover at all, just how Momma was treating her; like she no longer mattered, purposely waking up loudly, if she couldn't get any sleep stewing on her bed then Grover could wake up early and lose sleep too.

Momma asked if she was taking over for watch and Jani grunted, waiting for Momma to begin to rest in her own bed before obnoxiously prepping for the day. Creating noise as she threw potatoes into the coals and then dumped two logs on top of them. She pinged their iron pot on her knee and although it didn't hurt, Jani yelped, so both Grover and Momma could no longer attempt to sleep. After checking on her and seeing she was okay, Grover told Momma to go back to resting and that he was fully awake to keep watch if Jani needed to focus on breakfast.

The two young ones sat in silence, watching the potatoes until Grover pointed at the zip bag. Jani ignored him and he shrugged, and crawled over towards Momma's feet, sliding the zip bag back towards their seats. He unzipped it and Jani rolled her eyes, seeing he wanted to show her his trick. She continued ignoring him as she poked the potatoes and poked the coals, not wanting a huge smokey fire.

Grover tapped her on the shoulder so she could no longer ignore him. She rolled her eyes again as he overemphasized his magic trick, making the coin disappear from his hands. Jani feigned applause and tended to the potatoes, the two watching the tubers cook and be poked, cook and be poked.

After Jani's belly was full, she was more receptive to watching Grover's magic trick and she just couldn't see how he made the coin disappear, blaming it on not being able to see through the campfire's steamy smoke and only having early morning light. Crossing her arms just like she learned from her balance training with Momma Jani told him she knew magic wasn't real and Grover had laughed at her. Laughed!

After Momma got up and they set off for their day, Jani was astounded that Momma had shown her only daughter no extra affection or gratitude for taking that last watch, even if it hadn't given her much rest. Jani wanted instant forgiveness, deep inside she knew her mother had done no wrong, but she didn't want to be the one to bend first. Instead, she wanted to prove how mad she was to Momma and Grover so walked ahead of them all morning, quietly stomping along, thinking terrible thoughts until she realized she no longer heard them behind her. On a quest to be right Jani had walked past the site Momma had chosen for their lunch break and had to double back, feeling stupid for not paying attention. Jani traced her way back to them quickly, doubling back so she wasn't on her own for too long.

Arriving at their temporary site Jani found Momma and Grover each sitting on their rolled-up bedrolls, passing a can of expired vegetarian chili between them. Wanting to make everything how it should be, about her, she placed her bedroll beside Momma, she knew she had given into her urge to behave badly, forcing her way in between the two of them so that they would never forget her importance.

Grover handed Jani the can directly and Momma opened her stainless-steel bottle and took a sip of water, leaning back so that she could stretch out her back and chest. Jani held the can between her knees as she searched in the side pocket of her knapsack for her utensils, unwinding them and grabbing her spoon. She ate the remaining contents of the can while Momma dug through her duffel for the remaining potatoes Jani had cooked that morning.

While Grover and Jani unwrapped their potatoes Momma requested another magic show and took the zip bag out and tossed it towards Jani. Jani looked at her quizzically and Momma told her to pick a coin.

"C'mon darling, if we let him pick it, we know for sure he's tricking us," Momma explained and then winked at Jani.

Jani pulled apart the zip bag and shook it, taking out the biggest one, a thin, oblong silver colored piece of metal. Grover let out a small groan at that, saying he appreciated the challenge as Jani passed Grover the squished coin.

Grover successfully made the coin disappear and Momma and Jani kept asking how and for him to go again, and again, and again. Grover laughed and agreed until finally he pointed to the sky and told them that it was probably time to get on their way and Momma stood to attention and gestured with her index finger, miming a tornado to tell them to quickly get moving. Jani held the zip bag out to Momma and Momma told her that if she had room in her pack, she could keep it. As they made their way through the woods her heart swelled when Grover told her he'd show her again when they made camp, so she could watch slowly. He asked her if she wanted to learn, and Jani told him she had other drills to perfect so couldn't take on any new ones, totally serious.

Momma trailed slightly behind them for the rest of that day's travels, Grover and Jani laughing up ahead. Jani watched the coin disappear dozens of times before Momma got annoyed and told them to quit it and make camp. While they waited for their water to boil Grover repeated the magic trick again and again, and no matter how many times in a row she watched Grover, or how slowly she went, she could not figure out how he made the squished-out coin disappear. What irritated her most was that Grover watched her eyes the whole time, knowing what she was doing. That she was trying to learn his magic, his secret.

81: Then

Ana passed out the cutlery she had brought from home as Faith and Raven settled into their seats. Since the conflict with Raven over the dishes Ana had been contributing in this way. Less garbage created and fewer dishes brought home by Faith and Raven, who ate at their desks every other day of the week. It was just a couple of forks but Ana hoped it helped. At least they had both been delighted when they saw real silverware wrapped in cloth napkins that first meal they shared after Wayne had called Raven sexist.

Ana had decided she would wait until they addressed all the agenda items for the upcoming party before asking to speak to Raven privately and was taken off guard when Raven skipped referencing the agenda once they had all begun eating.

"This morning I saw Gabby in the restroom in tears," Raven announced.

"What was wrong?" Faith was so concerned stopped mid-bite to ask.

"She was so convinced she could prove herself to Paisley," Raven shared, shaking her head, "She didn't know Paisley doesn't notice shit and Basel was the one who wanted to get rid of her. Lucille is so young, Gabby still wanted to breastfeed. It's awful enough she has to return to work so soon if she wants to keep her job, but she's committed to Paisley and WWW just like we all are.

"She convinced her husband that returning to work would be worth it in the end and they bought a *thousand* dollar pumping machine, selecting the portable version just so she could return to her cubicle."

Faith let out a whistle at the expense and Raven nodded, continuing, "Gabby hasn't been paid these past few months and was crying so hard, worried about falling behind. With savings, her career, with her daughter's health and development. The pumping process is so complicated, and everything needed to be kept safe, hygienic, sterilized for the baby's safety. And Basel was not happy with Gabby's complicated.

"The breakroom is disgusting and there's been nowhere to wash her pump parts. Her husband had warned her she couldn't stay at WWW if pumping didn't work out. He's a doctor and had seen too many cases of babies getting sick from the bacteria which grows from the leftover moisture. Gabby was so upset because she doesn't think she'll be back next week."

"Ugh," Faith deplored, "I noticed Basel keeps going out of his way to make her miserable. He's usually never even around and for some reason he's been here before *and* after me all week, just to police Gabby, I'm sure."

Raven nodded, "Yeah, Gabby was crying about that too. There's no place for her to dry out her pump, she set up a little fridge under her desk for the baby's milk and he looked at her like she was disgusting for that. Basel managed to make Gabby feel ashamed for taking care of her baby!"

"Yeah, they really want her to use the bathroom, don't they?"

"Well, that is where she would be pumping if I didn't offer her my office before she got back," Raven pushed her plate away angrily.

"What?!" Ana exclaimed.

"Don't act too surprised," Raven admonished, "You've worked here long enough Ana."

"Yeah, but that's disgusting. Pumping where you…" Ana trailed off.

"That's what they think is okay," Raven seethed, "Acceptable."

"So, do you think she's going to quit?" Faith asked.

"I hope not but I *do* think she's going to quit. Basel doesn't want her around and Paisley doesn't seem to care or notice," Raven replied.

"I've seen her carry that sleek black tote in, is that where she keeps everything?" Ana implored.

Faith and Raven nodded.

"I have an idea," Ana began, "I know it may not be perfect, but we could at least try it, if Gabby wanted to that is."

"I'm listening," Raven tilted her head.

"We're used to hiding things, as women, right?" Anna proposed.

"Not me!" Faith exclaimed, "What you see is what you get! Guaranteed!"

"Really? You've never snuck into the bathroom with a tampon up your sleeve? Waited for everyone to leave before removing your maxi-pad, to be sure no one heard the sound?"

Raven smirked as Faith put up both her hands, "Okay, you got me, I can hide things sometimes."

"Exactly!" Ana exclaimed, "What if Gabby used that same discretion to wash and dry her items in the Executive Kitchenette?"

Raven frowned at this, and Ana continued to explain, "I could get Gabby Mr. Paisley's meetings for the day and she could sneak up to clean while I kept guard at reception. No one ever goes in there except for me. We could work out a signal so she knew when it was safe to come out of the kitchenette. Everything could air dry and I could package everything up so Faith could drop them off after her mail runs or I could leave them somewhere for Gabby to grab."

"I don't know," Raven said, clearly uncomfortable, "The kitchenette is off limits and that would result in Gabby being away from her cube for a long time, Basel has been watching her like a hawk."

"Okay," Ana considered this thoughtfully, "What if your office is the swap point? She pumps there and Faith and I do hand offs? I can clean the parts myself, if Gabby doesn't mind? I see the problem with that but in some ways that may be easiest..."

Ana watched Raven, certain she was about to say no, that Paisley's bathrooms and kitchen were just for him, that there were rules to follow.

"It would at least delay Gabby from quitting for a few days," Faith blurted out.

"I'll talk to Gabby first," Raven said with a cautious smile.

82: Now

Worried Jani's obsession with the magic coin would grow, Momma told Grover to put the squished coin back into the zip bag for the night and then gestured for Jani to hand it back once the coin had been deposited in it. Jani was careful to make no changes to her face, she knew Momma was about to give them an education and the last time Jani had told her she was too old for Momma's schooling it had not ended well.

The three of them continued setting up camp and prepping their rations for supper. When they began to eat, Jani found she was right. It was a night Momma felt like talking and teaching and she felt like teaching about the old days. She told them about how when she was in junior high, just about Jani's age on that night, how after school she never wanted to go home. Momma tried explaining sure there was stability, always food available on the shelves at the grocery store but not always at home for her and Jani rushed her through it, knowing she could talk to Grover later. Momma's Momma always made her sad.

After school Momma said she'd throw her bike on the school bus and ride her friends' routes home, imagining she lived in their houses, their own mommas having left snacks out for them, ready as soon as they threw their bikes in the yard and ran into the kitchen. Elyse and Mona. Momma and Mona always preferred heading over to Elyse's house after school, she had the best snacks. Momma went on about how Elyse's Momma would set up nacho bars with all the toppings or mini brunches for them, complete with mini-Belgian waffles, fresh strawberry syrup, and sparkling orange juice. Not only was the food at Elyse's house the best, she lived on a cul-de-sac, *I think you both know what those are,* and behind her house was nothing, no development at all. Lots of unused green space because no one wanted to live next to the train tracks and Elyse's uncle was the developer, so he was the one who scooped up the home at the end of the cul-de-sac, a gift for his sister and his brother-in-law.

"I always wanted to impress Elyse so bad," Momma told Grover and Jani, "I never quite understood why Elyse wanted to hang out with me. Jani knows my Momma didn't have even a tenth of what Elyse's Momma and Daddy did. I wore the same clothes on repeat, spot cleaning them because Momma only did the laundry when *she* didn't have anything to wear. Elyse's

Momma shopped at the mall for her, and Mona had such a funky sense of fashion. But somehow the three of us all became the best of friends."

The first, and only, spring of their friendship, after school the girls would eat at the breakfast bar and gossip about what happened at school that day and who liked who and who didn't deserve to be liked. At first Jani's Momma would try to do their dishes but Elyse's Momma got upset and asked Elyse to tell her to stop. She paid someone to do it a certain way Elyse had explained to Jani's Momma. Elyse never did her own dishes and Momma was the only one who ever did 'em in her own home. So, as hard as it was for Momma, she wanted to fit in and would join Elyse and Mona in leaving their messy plates, often with uneaten food on them, *can you believe it,* then grab some sodas from the fridge and run into Elyse's unfenced yard, never ending thanks to the unusable land, as deemed by these omniscient developers, as instructed by Elyse's Uncle.

As the weeks passed, the days grew longer, the girls grew older and as they got closer with one another, the girls grew more adventurous. *More reckless.* The summer after their freshman year, they had all the time in the world to explore. Jani knew Momma was sick of exploring.

Mona and Momma would wake up and bike miles upon miles to Elyse's and they'd laze the day away inside Elyse's beautiful home. When she had first moved into Reba Auntie's she couldn't believe how many rooms were in her home. There were more bathrooms than people who had ever stayed and that is how Momma had described Elyse's house to her and Grover that night. She told them how Elyse's dad was a bowler so her Uncle had built a bowling alley in the basement for his family. On the hottest of days that June they could choose to spend it soaking in Elyse's pool outside or inside playing billiards, table tennis, pinball, and of course bowling.

Momma laughed as she told Grover and Jani how the girls quickly grew bored with all the luxury.

"We decided we'd rather see how far it was to the train tracks that Elyse's dad claimed no one would want to live next to," she scoffed, rolling her eyes just as her daughter always did.

The first day they decided to make their way to the train tracks it was midday and so they didn't get too far, they stayed within the territory they were familiar with and on the way back to Elyse's house planned their exploration for the next day, they'd have breakfast with Elyse and then just start walking. Their cans of soda, wrapped in aluminum foil in an attempt to keep them cool. They got a little further the second day they tried but Mona said she didn't want to go any further, so they didn't. Elyse teased Mona for being afraid, but that day Jani's Momma had agreed with Mona, seeing how uncomfortable she was so Elyse dropped it.

"She pouted the entire way home though," Jani's Momma told the children, "Jani darling, she stomped ahead of us the whole way back to her house, Mona and I trailed behind her looking at one another. Neither of us had anything else going for us, especially that summer. My Momma worked all the time and didn't have any time or money for me. We got back to Elyse's house, and she stepped inside without us, she told us we could grab our bikes from the lawn, she wasn't feeling well and wanted to lie down."

Jani's felt her body temperature rise, ashamed she had acted the same way over some junk they had found on the ground.

Jani's Momma fidgeted, bouncing her left knee as she spoke, her left heel bouncing up and down off Mother Earth, "Mona and I grabbed our bikes and rode out of the very safe streets of Elyse's gated community, waving goodbye to Myles, who worked at the gate. He was always so nice to us, telling us how Elyse's Momma brought him lemonade almost every day. He was there every morning when we arrived and every day when we left. I wondered about that at the beginning of the summer and Elyse had told me he lived there with them. The staff at their gate, the community's country club, the landscapers, the maintenance staff..." Jani's Momma had trailed off and Grover and Jani looked at one another. There had always been talk about these kinds of places, bunkers underground that the richest and most powerful people had retreated to when the collapse became more and more real, accelerating, bringing with them people who were desperate, promised to do anything to survive. *Please, take me with you. I'll do anything you want.*

Grover looked worried and Jani almost asked Momma if she was ok but then her Momma began to speak again, sucking in her breath and then letting it out slowly, "They had *yoga instructors* living there. Lifeguards for anyone hosting a pool party. *Dog groomers!*" Jani's Momma doubled over in laughter, this time leaning forward. Momma was shaking, her head between her knees. When she came back up, sitting erect, Grover and Jani saw the tears running down her face.

Jani's Momma removed her spectacles and wiped her face with the mask that always hung on her neck. A cloth folded and knotted to serve many purposes. She composed herself and then continued, "Of course Myles lived there. He was their security guard. We left him and then when we were outside the gates, I asked Mona if she was ok, and she said she was fine. We didn't live near one another so rode home until our paths split, saying we'd see each other again in the morning.

"When I got to the gate of Deer Commons the next morning Myles said he couldn't let me in. I didn't even try to push it, I knew I didn't belong there. Every morning I always beat Mona there, her parents were around more so she didn't leave as soon as she had woken up. So, I hung out at the gate for her, Myles said that was ok. He had even passed me a little glass container telling me it was from Elyse's Mom.

"I hung out on the grass, next the road leading up to Myles's gate house, and laid my bike down on the grass, hoping none of the residents leaving Deer Commons would complain to Myles. I peeked into the glass container and saw her momma had packed me a little breakfast. She saw how I came over ravenous every morning and Mona mainly hung out while Elyse and I ate. It was then that I began to think Elyse was only my friend because she pitied me.

"Mona rode up and I gave her the scoop. I told her I would stay put, if she wanted to ask Myles to get in and I promised her I wouldn't be mad at her if Elyse did let her in but not me. Mona swore she wouldn't go in without me and left her bike on the grass with mine and then walked over to the gate house to speak with Myles.

"It didn't take long before she was walking back to me, shaking her head. I noticed she didn't have a glass container from Elyse's mom but didn't say anything. I just shoved mine in my knap sack, saving the bagel with cream cheese, fresh fruit, mini apple pastry, and orange juice for when I got back home. Mona told me that Myles wouldn't tell her anything either. Just that she wasn't on the list today.

"She told me what Myles had said when she asked him if we'd be on the list tomorrow, 'Well, we will have to find out tomorrow.'

"We both went back to the gate house together to thank Myles and then rode off again, this time heading to a park a little closer to Mona's home. All we discussed was what we should do. There was a big summer celebration for the three-day weekend and Elyse had promised we'd spend it together. It was a gigantic party for all the residents thrown by her uncle and we'd have so much fun. It was nothing I'd ever been a part of before. I'd never even been to school dances because my momma wouldn't pay for anything.

"So, we tried to figure it out. How to make it up to Elyse so we didn't miss their big party. Should we call her? Should we write? Should we call her mom? Should we give up? We analyzed it all and decided to ride our bikes back to Mona's house to call. Mona had a phone in her bedroom, and I didn't want anyone to know where I lived so I was glad when she volunteered her place, where I had only been a few times before.

"We decided we would call her on speaker phone, which meant that Elyse could hear both of us speak and she'd know we were calling her together," Momma explained to Jani, "We deliberated over this forever it seemed and then when we finally called, Elyse's mom answered and told us Elyse still wasn't feeling well and wouldn't be able to speak on the phone with us, hanging up before we could even say 'thank you'.

"I left Mona's after we decided we would show up again the next day. And we repeated our actions each morning for the rest of the week. On Thursday, Myles handed me the glass container with the leftover breakfast Elyse's mother had dropped off and asked if he could give me some advice.

"I nodded to him, already embarrassed at what he might say. I knew how pathetic I must have looked coming up to Elyse's gate house every morning for food that Elyse's mom would have no problem with throwing into the trash. Maybe he saw how I was using Elyse.

"'*Cindy, I've only worked here a few years, but I've worked around people like the Klines all my life. Why don't you leave Elyse and her family alone this weekend? This party will come around again and you don't need it to have fun with your friend.*'

"Myles paused then, and I grew frightened, the way he was looking around, how he didn't want anyone to hear what he was going to say to me, and even though I was scared, I took a step closer to the gate house and he leaned over the window, telling me, '*You say no to them and they don't like it; so, they misbehave. You should be proud if you say no to someone and they don't want to be your friend any longer think about that.*'

"I understood what Myles was saying but didn't believe it. It was the same old shit everyone said back then," Momma scrunched up her face and mimicked a shrill voice, toggling her shoulders in her faux reprimand, *"Be yourself and people will like you for who you are.* Well, I was poor and had no friends and had never had a summer as good as this one with Elyse at the top of the food chain. I had nothing. Not even a reliable Momma. Can you imagine?" Momma stared up at the stars, "Best friends with Elyse Kline. Walking in with her and Mona on the first day of school, everyone staring at us. The most popular girls in school.

"And so, I stood there, not knowing *what* to say. I just wanted everything to be ok," Momma laughed at the sky, "But I agreed to him. Showing up after Myles telling me I looked kinda pathetic would have looked even *more* pathetic. I promised him I wouldn't come back to the gate house until *after* the party. At the earliest. And I still remember what he said before I left.

"*Good, cause you'll be just fine without her. Friendship can't be this for that, can't be bought.*"

Jani's Momma took a break from her story telling, standing to stretch and shake out her body. She rolled out her neck and explained to Jani and Grover how she caught Mona on her way to Deer Commons and told her Myles' advice.

"Mona was glad to hear it. Her parents didn't like that she was spending so much time at the Klines' and thinking Elyse was more important than Mona's own happiness. We *always* slept over at Elyse's but that day we planned that I'd spend the night at Mona's.

"Elyse had a giant bedroom, a king-sized bed with beautiful handmade quilts, and her own phone line. Not just her own phone but her own phone line!" Momma could tell Jani and Grover were nodding along but didn't really understand, shaking her head at her daughter and the young traveler they had temporarily adopted she shrugged her shoulders, "You don't get it and that's your loss kids. But it was a big deal. We'd sit on her colossal bed and be so excited when the phone rang on Saturday nights, which it *always* did. So many of the boys wanted to be Elyse's boyfriend. So, we'd all hang out, having the most fun together, but when it came time to sleep, she'd set the phone on the nightstand next to her bed and that was the signal for Mona and I to move over to the floor. Cause we *always* slept on the floor. Which was FINE," Momma laughed when she saw Grover and Jani exchanging a look, "Alright, alright, I'm trying to help you understand. There would have been plenty of space for all three of us to sleep on Elyse's monster of a bed or for us all to sleep on the floor, but Elyse had to have things *her* way and it was her house, so Mona and I always agreed.

"Mona's bedroom wasn't nearly as big as Elyse's, but it was still so much nicer than mine. Grover, my momma and I moved a lot. And we got kicked out of a lotta places. Maybe that's why I'm so good at this now. Always moving.

"Mona's parent's house had a guest room with two twin beds, for when her cousins stayed over as they did quite often with both their parents working and being in school. Yeah, they didn't have fancy quilts, but they had the softest fleece blankets and Mona's parents had a ton of TVs because her dad was a television repairman or something. So, there was a little one in the guest room. It was kinda broken, but her dad had set it up so we could watch movies on it. We had a monster movie marathon, and since the tv was a little fuzzy, we had a blast scaring ourselves silly. We slept in our own beds in the guest room that night and we talked about Elyse a little, but it didn't take long for her to leave our minds.

"The next morning, we were hanging in Mona's living room watching reruns on tv and the phone rang."

"It was Elyse," Grover interrupted.

"It was Elyse," Momma confirmed, "We ran up the Mona's bedroom and put it on speakerphone. She was so curt with us. She must have been livid we didn't come over to beg Myles to let us in."

"So did she say sorry?" Jani fumed.

"She didn't have to," Momma said, "Mona acted like nothing was wrong. She wanted everything to go back to how it had been just a few days earlier just like I had when I was at the gate house with Myles. Neither of us minded that she called! We were happy!"

"So, what did she say?" Jani asked skeptically, not believing her Momma would ever put up with someone treating her so poorly, "Why was she calling?"

"*When do you think you will be over today?*" Momma gushed, with an unnatural smile on her face.

Grover and Jani both widened their faces, looking at each other in amazement. Disbelief that Jani's Momma, so fierce and tough could ever have been manipulated, bullied.

"I know, I know. That's why I'm telling you this story," Jani's Momma held her hands out in front of her, asking them to stop.

"Yeah, so we went over that afternoon, and Elyse wanted a sleepover because the party was the next day. Mona had to ask for permission, they had seen how upset she had been but also knew she had been talking about the Deer Commons party and her parents gave in, agreeing to drop her things off. When we were separated from Elyse, Mona told me she was nervous, her parents really didn't like that she was friends with Elyse, especially after Mona had been so upset, crying over Elyse dumping her that past week.

"I pretended to call home. I told Elyse I didn't have any clothes to wear for tomorrow so would have to bike home. I lied and said my Momma couldn't drop clothes off because she was working, and Elyse said she had a ton of clothes I could have that she had never even worn before. Still with the tags from when her personal shopper had bought them for her.

"Elyse then suggested Mona and I shop her closet, outfits we would wear to the party, to start our friendship fresh once again. And everything was perfectly normal that night. We talked about the party the next day, the outfits, me worrying that Mrs. Kline thought I was using her daughter. Was a leech.

"When Mona's parents stopped by, they were satisfied with Mona's demeanor and were glad to see Elyse's mom was home, that it wasn't Elyse in charge of *everything*. That night we had fun as always, and no, Elyse didn't offer the bed or to sleep on the floor, but we were fine with it. Both Mona and I were super tired, we had stayed up late the previous night with our monster movie marathon, and both made our way to bed before Elyse was ready. She wasn't happy with it, wondering why we didn't want to stay up late and talk.

"We were so tired and were finally able to convince her when Mona said we'd get up really early to make up for it. Make all the events planned for the celebration. That satisfied Elyse, I *thought*. But in my gut, I knew better. I didn't quite feel right at first so as tired as I was, I just couldn't sleep. And so, I just laid there, waiting for sleep to take over and I could hear Elyse stewing; I heard her deep, shaky breaths. I knew *it* from her breath. I looked over to Mona to see if she knew Elyse was upset too, to see if we should call Mona's parents to pick us up. They would have and the phone was right there, but Mona was totally asleep.

"And I joined her eventually only to be woken to Elyse cheerfully waking us up at four in the morning. We asked her what was going on and all she kept repeating petulantly was, *You promised! You promised! You promised!*," Mommas shrill voice got even scarier, "We didn't want to be on the outs with her again so got dressed, and then under Elyse's instruction, we went down quietly for breakfast," Momma mimed shushing Grover and Jani with an index finger.

"We didn't have any of the giggles we used to have. Elyse was acting like she was in command of us, pointing at things for us to pack in the waist packs we would carry with us when we went exploring. Riding bikes and exploring with backpacks on always got too sweaty, you know what that's like, plus we didn't want to ruin the cute outfits Elyse had picked out for us the night before.

"Some bananas and cans of soda. That is what we had packed," Momma had a look of consternation.

"Mona and I looked at each other at one point before Elyse slid the patio door open. We knew she was going to make us make it up to her before we could go to the party. To go exploring as far as she wanted to. When Elyse opened the patio door, we all walked past the pool, where we could have stayed until after the event had been set up, lounging in the heat of the sun, but we chose to follow Elyse. Well, she held the door open, and I took the first step past the pool."

83: When

"Seriously, no worries," Heath directed as Prem curled up on their couch. Riley's mom had gifted them a cordless phone, acting like it was an extra, that she had accidentally bought one too many for herself. Prem knew Riley was worried about her. That she'd become more scared than she had been before the interview. That she wouldn't leave their apartment until Manasa was found.

"Prem, I am wondering if you could confirm a lead, maybe come in," Heath continued in a whisper, "I heard through the grapevine that it's no secret Paisley's little brother has wanted to buy Mirror Marsh to expand Deer Commons. Without a body Manasa's estate is going to be in limbo, I hope she had a plan for taxes and maintenance, she's a woman with no family, no kids, as soon as she defaults, they'll swoop in, there'll be protests from other eco-warriors. A huge mess given Paisley's upcoming press briefing. They say he's gonna announce."

"Sure," Prem lied, sick to her stomach and ready to hang up.

"Great!" Heath exclaimed, "When you're in we can discuss what you'd need to submit for the pivot, we can't do a Month of Meatless Meals but thought you could run to the library and interview a few local garden clubs to come up with a plan to create a backyard habitat in a month. I wish we could pay you for your time, but this is the best I can offer, I've got a 1:30 open. See you then?"

"See you then," Prem said, listening to the staccato beep letting her know Heath had long ago hung up.

84: Now

Jani stood in between Jeff Uncle and Drishti on the first of the stone pavers. She couldn't believe it was real, the ancient stone monument was like nothing she had ever seen. The Legend of Eadwayne did not portray its beauty. The details imprinted on the stones, washed by Surya, covered with moss, sparkling through its age. Jani wondered if Drishti had seen photos of it in the Scriptorium before she had decided to leave. If she had shown Hans and that was why Hans let Drishti escape. And left it up to Jani to decide what to do with her.

"Watch your step, it gets real dark in places, and there's critters in here. Respect that we are in *their* home," Jeff Uncle made known.

They had left Jeff Uncle's cabin without proper gear. Jani couldn't believe Momma had admitted that to her and Grover around the campfire all those years ago and Jani had repeated Momma's mistakes.

"C'mon," Drishti said, "And remember what we said, watch out for snakes, not snake people. Just leave 'em alone."

Jani held her own snake's tongue, not snapping at Drishti, telling her she was more concerned about the snakes in Deer Commons than the snakes of Mirror Marsh. Jani held her tongue when she saw the old crone walk out from a room in the stone shadows.

85: Then

Ana stood over the coffee table; the local section of the *Gazette* hung loosely in her hands. She had just learned Rufus had been trapped by the biologists studying him. They had noticed he become ill and was rarely moving within his habitat. They had no trouble capturing him because the condition he was in had left him so lethargic and weak. Through testing, the biologists discovered Rufus had eaten something which had ingested rodenticide or maybe he had eaten something that had eaten something that had run across the poison.

"What are you doing?"

Ana jumped at Wayne's question, "Oh my, you scared me, Wayne!"

"What's going on?"

"What do you mean?"

"You look like you've seen a ghost. Or a snake!" Wayne snorted at his own 'joke'.

Ana walked back to her desk to check Mr. Paisley's schedule. Wayne was super early for his meeting with his brother and Gabby was still in Mr. Paisley's kitchenette. Gabby had refused Ana's offer to clean her pump and the accessories, explaining that she'd never be able to forgive herself if the worst happened, and her baby got sick from the parts not being properly dried and stored, she would blame Ana, her husband would blame them both.

"It's just better this way, even if it's a little harder to manage," Gabby had whispered apologetically the first time she snuck into the Executive Kitchenette.

Wayne was twenty minutes early. Ana tucked the local section under the planner which contained Mr. Paisley's schedule and shuffled papers around, pretending to work in case Gabby made any sound from within the kitchenette.

"Where's the local?" Wayne asked.

"Oh, here," Ana said as she pulled the local section back out and tossed it to him, where it landed on the floor.

Wayne didn't notice Ana's attitude, standing to grab the newspaper before settling back into the couch.

"This is hilarious Ana," Wayne chuckled, pointing at the black-and-white photo of Rufus, laying pathetically on his side, in a cage, "These idiot environmentalists are trying to prevent the sale of the land this idiot was found on! And the state is actually listening to them! MY land!"

Ana hadn't told Wayne about her moment with Rufus, how their eyes had locked, how Rufus had acknowledged her presence. How magical the moment had felt until Wayne came back to ruin it.

"What?" Ana choked on the word, remembering the feeling of that drive home, scared at how alone she was in the seat next to Wayne.

"Yeah, cause this stupid cat was found dying, and they said I didn't hunt the rattlesnakes but poisoned them. Disputing my bounty collection. Like they could ever find out!"

"Did you?"

"Did I what?"

"Poison the snake dens?"

"Of course, I did! The snakes are going to either poison us or we gotta poison them," Wayne scoffed.

Ana stood from her chair, placing her hands on her desk as she shouted, "They aren't poisonous you fucking idiot!"

The waiting room fell silent, and Ana felt the sweat beading on her upper lip.

Mr. Paisley opened his door and glared out into the waiting room, asking, "Is there a problem?"

Wayne stood from the couch and stomped over to his brother, "You better believe there's a problem. Get us some drinks and snacks Ahh-naa."

Mr. Paisley looked from Wayne to Ana but Ana had nothing to say.

"You heard the request Ana," Mr. Paisley encouraged.

Ana walked to the kitchenette and the two men stood outside the door to Mr. Paisley's office, she prayed they wouldn't see anything when she opened the door.

"Actually, let me help you Ahh-naa," Wayne commanded as he pushed the door to the kitchenette wide open.

Mr. Paisley's jaw dropped when he saw Gabby standing there with her tote bag, trying to look as small as she could.

"Out!" Mr. Paisley shouted to Gabby before turning his attention to his little brother and his executive assistant, "You two! In my office."

86: Now

Jani, Drishti, and Jeff sat on the stone floor of the stepwell, watching it lap across the edge of the first step. Jani's eyes kept flickering back to the old crone. Jeff Uncle had introduced her to Prem, who had simply nodded and said nothing. Jeff Uncle explained his understanding, that Prem had taken a vow of silence to protect Mirror Marsh, that at some point she had abandoned what was now Jeff Uncle's cabin, that she wished them no harm. Jani was at a loss. The ancient woman seemed harmless, skin and bones, and still Jani knew they should head back to Jeff's cabin, find some protection from her. She had told them what happened to Mona. What didn't make it to the Scriptorium. She told them her truth, why she was the only outsider to have ever been let inside the walls of Deer Commons.

"Momma said Elyse made her. That the snake had been sunning on the tracks. It wasn't enough that they had finally *made* it to the tracks. Elyse wanted more from them. The serpent warned them, made that rattling sound. Momma said Elyse challenged her first, told her to pick it up, throw it. Momma refused.

"She said Mona didn't even get close. It struck and got her. They couldn't help her."

"What happened," Drishti demanded.

"She said Mona survived, but it was bad. Had to be hospitalized for a long time. That Elyse told everyone Momma had ruined her life. Deer Commons was implementing even more restrictions. Curfews. Registrations. Mona's parents had gotten a lawyer and it was costing the Klines a lot. They paid Momma's Momma so she wouldn't say anything to anyone. I learned the word liability. The outsiders were the reason they canceled the celebration. They hired exterminators. Built extra walls. Their costs went up and Elyse let everyone know Momma had ruined her life…"

They sat in silence listening to the birds sing and the water lapping, each lost in their own thoughts.

Jani remembered arriving at Deer Commons. How she had been greeted.

"Step away from the gate. Deer Commons does not have capacity to take in outside, unvaccinated enemies."

"Warning. Retreat from the gate or you will be fired upon."

"Final warning."

It was fate that Commander Myles had been chosen as Commander and that he was inside the gate house that afternoon when Jani approached.

"You look just like her. Jenny?" Myles had asked.

She hadn't known what to say so said nothing.

"*Just* like her, it's incredible," Myles hesitated, "Elyse's family moved on long ago, one of those bunkers. But just in case anyone remembers, your mom... I had told her you needed new names."

"You can call me Jani," Jenny declared quietly, remembering how her Momma said the owners of The Chai House had called her Rani when she was little. Jenny Rani becoming Jani Rani over the years. Momma had said there may be some good people here. They could follow the train tracks, try.

Jeff Uncle looked over to Jani, he had remembered the incident involving Jani's Momma. Seen the girls at the gate house, riding their bicycles on the trails as he walked with Lara after work. Over the years it had come together. He still felt Lara's skin in his hands some nights.

He remembered how he had held Lara's hands across the dinner table at the club house that evening the Summer Celebration had been canceled. Not everything had been called off, they still dined at the club house that night. How they were grateful for the protection Deer Commons offered. How they didn't have to do a thing except stay inside. There was someone to take care of everything.

Drishti thought about the Guardians, the Medics, the Cooks, the Mechanics, how they followed orders without ever thinking on their own. Just rushing from house call to house call so that whomever The Council valued could stay safely inside.

87: When

"Why would I want to move out there?"

"I know it's a big decision Prem."

"It's an awful decision."

"We've been through so much, the lawyers, the cops, the bureaucracy. If we stay in the city, everywhere you go…"

"People will talk. People will stare," Prem finished Riley's thoughts as she reached behind to scratch her scalp, the itchy dry patch had snaked up her neck. Prem no longer cared that Riley had seen her scaly skin. She refused Riley's help, no longer massaging expensive salves into her skin, doing everything she could to stop their spread.

"Maybe you could make a list of what stresses you out about living in the city and what would stress you about moving to Mirror Marsh. But I want you to know I need a change. Manasa wrote me and the engineering firm into her estate years ago. You've been through the investigation *with* me Prem. I had nothing to do with her, it was just by chance that she read that article. I didn't even remember it until Raven explained."

"She's manipulating us. Cursing us with a burden."

"Prem, how would she have known we were roommates, much less in love."

Prem flipped in their bed, turning her back to Riley's belly. Exposing her scales.

88: Now

Jeff Uncle had insisted on showing Jani the stone platform overlooking the stepwell. He lit a torch as he told her, "You never know what you'll see." Prem had followed along behind them. Jani wondered if she was more animal than human now. Jani had felt that way when she had approached Myles at the gate house so many moons ago. She could recognize that feral feeling.

There were birds everywhere, it surprised Jani they weren't engraved on any of the stones. Prem gestured for Jani to settle into the throne, not swatting away the cobwebs and insects, the debris that hand landed on the seat through the open design.

The platform was dimly lit, Jeff Uncle had lit another torch and hung both in place. They listened to the song of Mirror Marsh echo through the chambers of the stepwell. Prem sat on the stone floor, resting her back against one of the benches so that she could face the breeze that flew through the open space.

"It feels wrong that I am sitting here," Jani mentioned as she began to stand up.

"Please," Jeff Uncle reasoned, "Let's take a little rest here. It was built for us."

"Maybe that's because whoever is sitting there needs to tell the Legend of Eadwayne," Drishti playfully said.

Jani considered this and looked over at Prem, "This is the version Reba Auntie told me."

Eadwayne, a trader of goods, had been traveling for days without a safe night of sleep. His aching stomach had only been eased with some berries and roasted seeds; snacks that had been packed by the kind family who had allowed him to spend the night under their roof a few nights before.

The trader knew it was unlikely he would find sound sleep out in the open, there were tales of warlords, women of the night, and thugs looking to rob men just like Eadwayne after all, but eventually he pushed the rumors from his homeland, the city, aside and drifted asleep under the cold drizzle of rain. He had tossed and turned until he fell into slumber, trying with all his might to push the thoughts that kept him awake away with his family's mantra, *it's just business*. Eadwayne yelped in his sleep, he had dreamt the dream he always had. He was floating above a pit of darkness, deep as the night. There was a woman by his side, she had helped him, she wanted the best for him. He loved the shape of her body, the curves, the movement of her hair. It was hypnotizing. The lovely beauty smiled down at him and opened her palms, showing him all there was in this realm. Eadwayne bent down to see what composed the darkness, a darkness deeper than the night he traveled under a new moon, and when he floated as close as he could try to the opaque shadows, he saw dry, flaky, snake skins float right past his face. Afraid the snake skins were a sign serpents were in the deep, he tried floating away but found himself getting closer to the dark pool of water, molted snake skins floating on the top. He knew to touch one meant death. The woman was upset with him. He couldn't reach for her, she was always out of his reach, he couldn't explain, he couldn't leave, so like he always did Eadwayne reached for one of the snake skins and immediately woke up, knowing in the pit of his stomach that his own family were in a way warlords, women of the night, and thugs; they were just a bit more sophisticated. That it was time for Eadwayne to accept he was the same.

Eadwayne always woke up wanting more from the woman who led him to the darkness. He was in love with her, thinking of her during his waking hours but he could never remember anything about her. What was her intrigue? Why was she always on his mind?

*

Eadwayne had been wondering if his elder brother Whylerd had issues with the way their parents did business like he did. If they caused Whylerd to have nightmares too. If Whylerd worried about their little sister Agniss like he did, who their parents may marry her off to. He couldn't talk about things like that with Whylerd, he couldn't talk to Whylerd at all, he was one of the most sought-after business counselors in their empire. He thought about saving his sister, moving her far away from the city, their mother had been courting her to men twice and even a few times *three* times her age, so Eadwayne wondered upon sending her away, it was becoming fashionable to send daughters to boarding schools to learn basic accounting and conversational skills, but Agniss was the only daughter of their family. It was important to their parents that Agniss complete her duty and strengthen business ties to help her brothers. They each had a role in building their wealth. It was their family's duty to the empire.

Eadwayne laid still, waiting for the first daylight to break as he thought of how scared he was to talk with his family, to ask Agniss if she'd want to go to boarding school, if she'd want to move away but didn't think they could discuss Eadwayne's issues with their business, that Agniss would ever leave the comforts of their city, in fact other than Eadwayne, who was sent on these treasure missions to complete *his* duty to the family, they rarely even left their gated castle, the protection beyond their moat.

His father was such a powerful man and Eadwayne was afraid of him, scared to ask his father if business could ever be done another way even if his father ever made such time for him. Lately when he was home, he drowned his sadness by walking about the castle and putting out the torches in his family's quarters, worried that one of their servants would be injured, he was always sure to leave the torches in their halls lit. His passive lesson made no impact, it seemed his family weren't bothered at all by the darkness.

One morning at breakfast Eadwayne pointed the problem out, "Has anyone else been finding the torches in their quarters put out? It's become quite a nuisance."

"Oh, you silly thing," his mother marveled, "Just ring for the servants, let them stumble in the dark lighting them."

"They're better at it than us anyway," Agniss interjected, knowing Eadwayne didn't ask for servants in his quarters. She, like they all did, didn't understand why he allowed his servants so much sleep.

He sometimes wondered if his family could survive working as servants in their own castle, if they could withstand listening to the conversations that they had if roles were reversed, listening to the wealthy complain that the poor folks owed them and the rural folk owed them so much more. Whenever Eadwayne felt awful for taking advantage of someone, he would remember what his father had told him, 'It's just business.' After Eadwayne had embarrassed Whylerd one too many times, he had a rare infection of empathy, seeing how Eadwayne struggled with their father's justification he offered him another, 'It's just how the Earth is. If it wasn't us, it would be someone else. It's much better that it's us, you understand that Eadwayne?'

Eadwayne let Whylerd clap him on the shoulder and returned the gesture with the same thin lipped smiled he had given Sabrina, the woman who packed his food, a few nights earlier. Sabrina, who ran her household, hadn't wanted him to come inside, he had heard her snap at her husband how hard it was to feed their own, but Eadwayne eventually won her over, telling her stories from the city and about the charity of his church. She hadn't looked up to see Eadwayne's thin-lipped smile when she insisted he take the food she had packed for him, shoving the snacks tied away in a cloth rag into his hands while she looked at their feet. 'I'm ashamed we can't offer you more,' Sabrina confided before turning to walk back into her kitchen. The rest of her family saw the trader off, their young children making Eadwayne sick to his stomach when they pushed their palms against one another and bent their heads in a bow, a sign of respect before shouting, 'Safe travels! Please come visit us again after your family has built their new church here!'

Eadwayne hoped he never saw Sabrina and her kind family ever again, he would lie to his own family, they would never know he had stopped there or about the wealth Sabrina's hick family didn't even know that they had. Not just their fertile soil. Sabrina's husband had naively traded rare seeds for an old kettle, an item Eadwayne had taken from the family he had last stayed with, who had also traded rare seeds, those that could bear fruit and vegetables from the seeds they carried inside, not aware of the devastation that had occurred to the farms across the empire, the ones which were located closer to the city and Eadwayne's family's church. The new progress was going well for those whom it was meant to go well for, the taxes implemented by those with power who put into law the types of seed which could be sown. The same types of people who were his distant relatives and who his mother wished her son to be coiled tightly with one day, whether through marriage or through his service to the church. Eadwayne thoroughly understood his family's expectations and worried about disappointing them, unable to nest comfortably so close to the empire's wealth and power.

It's just business.

*

Day, night, and the hours in between, Eadwayne agonized over taking advantage of these ignorant hicks. They did not know that in a few seasons they wouldn't be able to continue farming without depending on the empire, even the charity of the churches they promised did not include seeds. In just a few years these people would have nothing, especially if they kept giving away their seeds, their secrets. But as sad as Eadwayne felt about the plight of these rural strangers, he mourned even more having to watch his elder brother get to stay in the city, Whylerd wining and dining those their family wanted to sell this information Eadwayne was collecting to. The farms and settlements that were independent, wealthy with seed. Eadwayne's family had promised him he wouldn't have to do this work for too long, be surrounded by those ignorant rural type folks, to keep returning to the city that darker brown from spending so much time with the rural folks' warrior God, Surya, where it would take months of isolation after his return to be deemed fair enough, clean enough to wine and dine with his elder brother, to take credit for the intel his family sold in front of those his family wanted to be closest to. Just in time to be sent out again.

Eadwayne had liked every single hick he had ever met more than his own family and couldn't understand why that was. The rural folk his family discussed with disdain seemed to reciprocate Eadwayne's feelings, being kinder and more accepting of him than his own blood. Which led Eadwayne's thoughts to even worse places. His family's hunts, always leaving the animals chased and killed to waste. Eadwayne often thought of the time his father commissioned an artist and once his portrait had been captured with the animal he had murdered, he left the sitting, simply leaving the body on the ground, explaining condescendingly to the shocked artist that the animal would return to the Earth. Through Eadwayne's travels to find the remaining self-sufficient farmers, the rural folks who still had healthy seed remaining, he began to view his family's hunting with disgust. They only did it because they were bored. Eadwayne had learned the practices of the ignorant hicks, how they never killed unless they absolutely had to, if something devastating had happened to their crops, if a sudden need for fur or leather was needed, and it only happened if the clan voted so. He had witnessed votes where mothers, just like the one who had packed his snack sack, had stood holding hands with one another. Their voices shook as they proclaimed that they would help the clan obtain the materials by going without, by working a little harder. To take a life before they exhausted all potential solutions would return upon the clan with consequences they could never dream up. This was one of the things that all the people of the city laughed at about the ignorance of hicks. They truly believed Mother Nature was an accountant, keeping a tally of credits and debits of their moral behaviours.

'The most curious thing,' Eadwayne's mother had clucked upon his first return, 'Is their belief of Ahimsa. They're willing to suffer because a voice in their heads tells them they must love all beings as they love themselves?'

'Yes Ammi,' Eadwayne had replied, scrutinizing his mother's reaction as he hated being on her bad side. She had favored Whylerd, her eldest son, always and only showed kindness towards Eadwayne if he was hesitant to help expand their family's fortunes. If she needed something from her youngest son.

She had dismissed Eadwayne with a dip of her chin and Eadwayne stood still for a moment. He had wanted to continue the conversation but was smart enough not to do so. As he returned to his father's library, he thought of how angry his mother would have become had he shared his thoughts.

Yes Ammi, and the reason they were so kind to me and shared their home, nourishment, and values is because they believe the cause of all suffering is human greed and possessiveness. Ahimsa is not easier for them, they are just far more skilled at resisting cowardice.

Oh, Ammi would have punished Eadwayne for weeks if he had said that. So Eadwayne walked the coward's walk to his father's library where he was ignored by his family until it was time to ask Eadwayne for his help once again. To leave the comforts they never would.

On his last few travels, he had thought about wandering off, never returning to his family but couldn't do that to them. They had provided for him after all. So now it was time for him to provide for them. Ammi had told him that was *his* karma. One day he would have sons who would do the same she told him, not knowing Eadwayne would hate to force such ambition upon another, most especially his children, his blood. The rural folks had woken him up to that, the one choice he could make was to not cause suffering. Even if that meant keeping his mouth shut towards Ammi.

Eadwayne was ready to start his day and so stood after his night of restless sleep, the warrior Surya had made his appearance, bright and causing the world to smell fresh all around him. He noted where the sun was and began upon his way, in just two days he would near the inn where he could arrange a ride back into the city. In less than a week he would be sleeping in his own bed after being the honored guest in his own home, at dinner. He hummed the empire's anthem, a tune to marched along to and keep pace as he thought about what Ammi would have the servants cook up, lost in his thoughts about delicious khana when he heard a call for help.

Eadwayne looked up and saw a young man limping his way. Eadwayne cautiously placed his hand on the blade he kept in his vest as he waved with the other.

'I'm begging ya for help,' the young man howled, 'I walk alongside me mule and twisted me ankle and now he won't walk a step further.'

'I don't see how that has anything to do with me, I can send help once I get where I'm going,' Eadwayne replied.

'Ahh, man, I'm begging ya,' the young man bawled, tears in his eyes, 'Ya can have an item of your choosin' from me cart if ya just get me to the stepwell.'

Eadwayne was now interested in helping this young man, the stepwell was a legend in the city. The empire had many tales of the wealth to be found near the stepwell, so much waterfowl that could be hunted and sold, beavers for their furs, plants that seeded on their own, but it was a magical oasis, no one from the empire had ever found it or could ever find it because it was concealed by magic. Cultists that worshipped a Goddess who protected the rural villagers from the pandemics that plagued the cities had cast special magics so that anyone wishing the creatures of the marsh harm would never be able to locate it. Eadwayne had tried to find this hidden realm but not one of the rural folks he ran across ever spoke of it when he was on his travels. His parents and their friends jabbered on and on about it as the perfect place for a trading post which Eadwayne found ridiculous. *If it could be found.* If no one could find it, no one would travel there was Eadwayne's observation, which he kept to himself.

According to those who knew much more than Eadwayne, it had been built specifically for travelers to always have fresh water and there were guardians who provided medical care and meals for those who may need that type of support. However, tales from the city warned, travelers would never stay the night, at dusk the guardians became cultists, creatures of the night who swept out everyone who did not commit to protecting the stepwell for eternity. Eadwayne couldn't believe his parents believed this tale; if such a place existed, their empire would have taken it by force long ago.

'Curious accent,' Eadwayne cautiously began as he took in the young man in front of him, 'Where are you from?'

'Aye, I'm from 'ere and the sisters sent me to Deer Commons for trading. Everyone calls me Sam. They send me where I need to go when they need help. And will you help me?'

Eadwayne thought on this, whether to believe the stories of shapeshifters at the stepwell. If they were true, a shapeshifter stood before him. If the stories were false Eadwayne would lose an opportunity for greatness. For him and his family.

'Let's check out your mule, maybe you can get home on your own,' Eadwayne pointed out.

'I appreciate any help my ser.'

Eadwayne dismissed the teenager's use of sir and the two walked slowly towards the mule, who seemed to relax once he saw Eadwayne was with Sam. There seemed to be no issue with the mule until Eadwayne turned to walk on his own. The mule then stubbornly stopped again, and Sam called out for Eadwayne.

"He won't let me travel alone if I'm hurt," Sam apologized.

'So, we'll walk together?' Eadwayne suggested, thinking he would at least be able to mark a course from the stepwell to the inn. His parents would have to favor him more than Whylerd then.

'The quickest route is up a steep hill, for that I'd need to dump some of these goods and ride in the cart,' Sam offered, embarrassed.

Eadwayne peeked in the cart and saw it was full of vegetables and bound books.

Sam shrugged, telling Eadwayne, 'I just make the trip, I don't even know what I'm givin' or gettin'.'

Eadwayne told Sam, 'The contents are surprising, but I'm mainly surprised that you get your mule to carry such a heavy load.'

'That's why the in-charge only allows use of a mule.'

'What do you mean?' Eadwayne asked.

'Cuz a mule stops when she's tired.'

Eadwayne was such a good traveler because he never showed his judgement of the hicks' customs and values, no matter how surprisingly backwards they may be. And so, Eadwayne simply smiled at Sam through the ridiculousness of what he had just said and said, 'We'll take the long way then.'

He'd still be asleep in his bed in less than a week.

*

Sam held out his arm, signaling to Eadwayne to not move any further. Sam stretched out his arm and Eadwayne followed the line Sam's pointer finger was creating. Eadwayne saw a woman sitting underneath the oak tree Sam had brought to his attention. Eadwayne looked at the teenager and saw Sam was now pressing his pointer finger to his lips, the signal to stay quiet. Sam acted out, without actually moving, tiptoeing without sound and Eadwayne understood his instructions but had no guarantee about the volume levels of Sam's squeaky cart or his mule with many complaints, Moonu.

Sam, Moonu, Eadwayne, and the cart moved slowly through the meadow. Sam had explained that they must stay on the paths and not create new ones for that would destroy any of the homes of the beings that lived there or further harm the ecosystems of the marsh. Eadwayne respected the practices of the people who lived at the stepwell although this put their path closer to the yogini meditating underneath the oak tree.

They passed her in silence and Eadwayne noticed she was seated directly on Earth. This surprised him as the ground here held so much more water, he thought that she must be under some sort of punishment. Eadwayne stood in his tracks and slipped his bedroll off his shoulder and released it from his pack. Sam and Moonu watched with their jaws open as Eadwayne knelt to the Earth and presented it gently to the yogini. Eadwayne hopped in surprised when he saw the yogini had opened her eyes.

'This is generous however I did not ask for this gift,' the yogini asserted to Eadwayne.

'Yes, but I thought you may have more need for it than me, right now.'

'Oh, so you sought chivalry,' the yogini confirmed.

'If anything, *you* are being chivalrous,' Eadwayne shyly said, 'It is one less thing for me to carry on my journey.

Maybe you can give it to someone who needs it, or I can also take it back.'

The yogini thought upon Eadwayne's offer before deciding on her choice, 'We believe in reciprocity. And we can't exist in this world without causing some harm. I shall return your offering with what you desire most, information collector. When the time comes, remember everyone here has two names.'

The yogini blinked her eyes shut and bowed her chin, dismissing Eadwayne and ignoring the bedroll beside her.

When the yogini was far behind them Eadwayne finally asked Sam if he and Moonu had more than one name.

'Of course we do,' Sam laughed. Eadwayne watched as spit flew from Sam's mouth and saw Moonu had been watching that too. He swore Moonu was laughing too. It had to have been real when Moonu joined in, answering, 'Two names, just like you Ser Eddie!'

*

Moonu and Eadwayne stood on the pavers leading to the stepwell oasis. Sam had insisted they wait as sunset was nearing and visitors were not invited to stay overnight. Sam would ask the sisters of the stepwell if an exception could be made for Ser Eddie. If they didn't allow him in, Eddie would probably be safe sleeping near the stepwell but outside. Still, it was better to ask if the sisters would allow an exception. The sisters did forgive, but it was always better to have their permission Sam had recommended.

Eddie leaned against Sam's cart as he waited for his new friend to return, inhaling the warm air around him. Something about it relaxed him in a way that he hadn't felt before. His mind drifted to the idea of staying here forever, knowing it was ridiculous, he hadn't even stepped inside and was willing to abandon his family over a hidden, magical oasis. He heard Moonu snortle and snapped awake. He shook his head, aghast that multiple nights in a row of poor sleep had led to him falling asleep while standing.

He looked over to Moonu and saw he seemed to be arguing with something or someone on the ground. Eddie looked down and saw a small brown creature with wings and large ears. Moonu was arguing with a brown bat! Eddie held back a scream to eavesdrop. In the city, they chased away bats for the diseases they brought.

'You promised me you'd help Moonu!' the brown bat exclaimed.

'Moonu doesn't have any say in trade. He just pulls the cart,' Moonu explained logically.

'Well tonight was special for Saffy! A full Blood Moon, you know I wanted to make it special.'

'It'll be special, you'll be together,' Moonu shrugged.

'You don't want the bats against you on a full Blood Moon,' the brown bat said in a way that Eddie found threatening.

'Why would I ever want the bats against me?' Moonu pondered.

'What sorts of things might Saffy like?' Eddie asked.

'He's with us today,' Moonu exclaimed, nodding his muzzle in Ser Eddie's direction when the brown bat began flapping his wings, clearly upset.

'I'm just trying to help,' Eddie apologized, 'The less I have to carry to the inn, the better.'

'You're going to which inn?' the brown bat asked.

'How about introductions first? I'm Eadwayne, a trader from the city.'

'Ahh, the big city,' the brown bat said with disgust, 'Rick.'

'Glad to meet your acquaintance, Rick. Now tell me about your Saffy.'

'Well, she ain't mine yet!' Rick scoffed, 'That's my issue with Moonu. He *knew* today was a special date.'

'Well, who cares what I know,' Moonu stated, without emotion.

'You're looking to impress Saffy,' Eadwayne considered, 'How about this?'

Rick looked at the cloth Eddie had laid on the ground, 'We can eat nuts and berries whenever we want.'

'Okay,' Eddie said, gathering his snack before rooting through one of his bags, 'How would Saffy like this?'

Rick looked at the gold ring, shaped as a snake, in awe, 'This is *exactly* what Saffy would want. But how could I pay you for this?'

'You don't have to pay me anything,' Eddie said, 'I'm a guest in your home for now and owe you.'

'Moonu, would you hang on to this for me? For Saffy?' Rick asked.

Moonu nodded his head and Rick watched as Eddie tied the ring to Moonu's mane, asking, 'Are you sure Saffy will be able to get the ring out from this knot?'

Moonu snorted in response, 'Like Saffy needs help from anyone to do anything.'

'Thank you both. Information collector, for your kindness I must offer a gift in return. Saffy misses her jewelry and will be so pleased,' Rick paused, unsure if he should continue, 'If you make it down the corridor, don't stay to dine. The King will issue an invitation, but it doesn't mean you must accept it. Saffy, Moonu, and I have witnessed too many tricked by the mirage. Nothing can be so easy; you must know that Ser Eddie.'

And when dusk fell, Rick introduced Saffy to Ser Eddie. The raven's ability to unknot Moonu's plait to obtain Rick's gift did not shock Eddie. He was shocked at the teardrop that fell from the raven's eye as she held the ring with one claw and the embrace of Rick's wing on top of her own.

*

Eddie and Sam walked into the stepwell together, Rick's warning to Eddie heavy on his mind. Sam led Eddie upstairs to a large stone platform, announcing that Eadwayne could take a seat wherever he'd like while he waited for the Mother of the Marsh to receive him. As Eddie looked at the stone benches, deciding where to sit, he felt as though he was within an incredibly sacred place. He listened to Sam quickly explain that Eddie had been granted a rare exception to the Sisters' rule, because it was a Full Blood Moon they felt a level of protection from outsiders they normally didn't have. Eddie watched Sam head back downstairs to let the Mother of the Marsh know Eddie was waiting, whenever she was ready to receive him. Eddie felt as though his parents had been right, the stories from the empire were true. He had been left alone in the cultists' temple, this place was nothing like his family's church and these Sisters must worship something and someone else.

Eddie turned around to take a seat and where just moments ago the only items in the room were two empty stone benches, the room was now almost completely full. Between the stone benches was a banquet table, and at the end, a red, plush throne faced Eddie. The table was full of all of the foods his father, mother, and elder brother had described to Agniss and him upon returning from the fanciest of banquets. An entire suckling pig, with a bright red apple in its mouth, bowls upon bowls of fresh fruit, candied, mashed, and curried potatoes, breads, butters, pickled onions, peppers, chilis, and mango, crackers, and cubed cheeses.

There was a steam rising from the table as though it had just been freshly delivered from the kitchens of the stepwell. Except Eddie knew no such kitchen could exist here. It was simply a stopping point for travelers who needed fresh water. If the empire could not afford such a meal for Eddie how could the Mother of the Marsh possibly afford to do so?

Eddie held his breath when he felt a presence enter the room and sit at the velvety, red throne. He let out a hiss of air as he saw just as there were no beings seated at the benches, there was no one seated in the throne. He noticed there were tapestries on the wall which hadn't been there before. He thought.

Eddie walked around the banquet that had been arranged and examined each tapestry, a scene of a Sister of the Marsh with the Mother of the Marsh displayed on each one. The Mother always wore a bright red sari and held a snake in each hand as though they were lightning bolts and the snakes were happy to be held by the Mother. Each Sister seemed to have their own powers as well, in one tapestry Eddie could see the power of one Sister's open mindedness and another's ability to lead a team. In another Eddie saw a Sister show forgiveness and while another showed bravery. He saw the near perfect depiction of the yogini he had met earlier under a tree, her action towards transcendence matched with another Sister's action towards justice. After carefully examining each tapestry, hoping it would help him when he met the Mother of the Marsh, Eddie turned to see a large black cat seated in the throne.

'You didn't hear me come in?' the cat purred.

'My apologies,' Ser Eddie bowed in respect, 'I..'

The black cat cut Ser Eddie off with a sneeze, 'I'm joking. I'm a hunter, you would only hear me if I wanted you to hear me. Care to join me Ser Eddie?'

Ser Eddie approached the cat while looking at the floor, remembering Rick's warning about the King. As Ser Eddie kneeled at the black cat's throne he said, 'Thank you my King. I would love to join you but I must meet with the Mother of the Marsh before I travel back to my home.'

'How about just one bite?' The King hit the leg of the table with their fluffy black tail and the apple fell from the pig's mouth into Ser Eddie's lap.

'May I take this to offering to the Mother of the Marsh?'

'Alas, the Mother provided this meal so is no offering to her. She is ready for you. Go on your way,' the King of the Marsh dismissed Ser Eddie as they began cleaning their paw, 'I'm surprised you didn't want to dine with me. I rather like being surprised.'

The King hopped off their throne and walked towards Ser Eddie who remained kneeling while the King continued their monologue. Ser Eddie froze as he felt the King's whiskers brush up on him.

'Don't worry Eadwayne,' the King said before strolling away, 'I know a little magic too.'

Ser Eddie's gaze followed the King, watching them jump on to the stone ledge and then off of it, skipping the route which took the stairs. Eddie walked to the ledge and saw the sun had fully set and when he turned around the room was exactly as it had been when Sam brought him to it. No table full of fresh khana, steaming with aromas, and no red velvet throne. Ser Eddie stood frozen in wonder as Sam walked up from the stairs.

'Ya coulda sat on one of da benches while ya waited,' Sam said cautiously, 'You're me guest, we didn't expect ya to stand after such a long journey.'

'Yeah, that was a little weird,' Ser Eddie agreed.

As the two men walked down to the stepwell Ser Eddie realized he could see clearly in the pitch dark of the stairwell.

Ser Eddie emerged from the stairwell grateful for the King's gift. The glow of the Blood Moon provided more light than usual, but he wouldn't be able to see at all if that proper black cat hadn't enhanced his vision.

Ser Eddie followed Sam to the edge of the stepwell, and it seemed as though the Mother of the Marsh seemed to be floating in the center of it. His nightmare had come true.

'Mother, this is Ser Eddie who helped me back to Mirror Marsh when Moonu was worried I would not make it on me own.'

'Step forward Ser Eddie,' the Mother of the Marsh instructed.

Eddie took one small step forward and realized he was entirely alone. Sam had shifted into the shadows and Eddie then realized an audience had gathered there which Sam had joined when dismissed by the Mother. Many animals of the marsh stood in the dark, with Sam and a few other humans. Eddie could make out Moonu and the King but did not recognize anyone else.

'You arrived with an invitation. Are your intentions pure?' the Mother of the Marsh asked Eddie.

'My intentions?' Ser Eddie stuttered.

'Yes, why are you here today?'

'Why I helped Sam back home, he insisted I stay.'

'He insisted because you needed something, no?'

'I only came because I wanted to help.'

'Help,' the Mother of the Marsh scoffed, 'Like you help the families who gave you their seed?'

Eddie patted his sack; it hadn't left his sight since before he met Sam. Panicking, he looked into the shadows for help.

Hearing no response from Ser Eddie, the Mother of the Marsh spoke again, 'I didn't need to look in your pack to know your plans for the seeds you've collected. Would you take the seeds from the marsh on your way?'

'No, you don't understand,' Eddie sputtered.

'I do,' the Mother of the Marsh gently explained, 'I don't need your excuse when I have your vision.'

Ser Eddie didn't know what to do. The light of the Blood Moon was growing brighter, and he grew fascinated by the Mother of the Marsh's body, her curves and belly, the outline of her hips reflected on the water. Dancing. But most, Eddie couldn't stop bringing his eyes up to her hair, its movement was hypnotizing.

'You think you should wander from your home, and that is what led you to me,' the Mother of the Marsh claimed, 'Come closer so I can see you.'

Ser Eddie took a step forward, down into the stepwell.

'There you go,' the Mother of the Marsh spoke kindly, 'Do you think you deserve to stay here information collector?'

Ser Eddie kept walking forward, unable to control his feet, step by step, he moved deeper into the well.

'Your family would hurt you to hurt others, for their own gain,' the Mother of the Marsh continued, 'They create walls and moats to keep the people you steal from out of their empire yet judge me for keeping my home safe?'

Eadwayne felt his cheeks burn with shame, the Mother of the Marsh was correct. He found himself thinking of no longer fighting the magic propelling him forward, down into the stepwell.

'I offer you a place in our home, in our family, and a purpose,' the Mother of the Marsh declared.

'A place to stay?' Ser Eddie chattered, frightened at his feet wanting to move down the steps. He wasn't sure he was ready to leave his family. His city. The empire was the only home he had ever known.

'A place to be with us,' the Mother of the Marsh corrected.

Ser Eddie woke up from his trance, believing the Mother was trying to haggle with him as he had haggled with the rural folk for information, for their seeds. He tried his best to resist the Mother, forcing himself retreat backwards up the steps, hoping to keep distance away from the ghost which hovered above the pool.

Eadwayne could not even fight her magic enough to stop walking forward.

'Oh, you cute thing,' the Mother of the Marsh laughed. Eddie looked back and saw the shapes in the shadows had moved closer and were now framing the top step of the stepwell. Each of the beings the Mother protected.

'Please help me! I appreciate you opening your home to me but my mother will be so worried if I don't return,' Eddie cried out to Sam.

Again, the Mother of the Marsh laughed, 'Your mother doesn't worry about you now but will if you won't return, you are correct. She wants the name of the landowners who use their own seeds. Without your return your elder brother will have to follow your steps. Not these ones of course.'

Eddie felt her pull and moved further down into the stepwell. The water was well above his waist.

'Is there anything I can do? Please, you must think of my family! My little sister. The empire is only collecting their information, their seeds for their own good,' Eddie pleaded.

'Oh, baby Eadwayne. How I wish nothing but love for you. The love I have for myself if the love I extend to you and yours. This is our fate.'

'Please, let me live.'

'Oh, but you will live Ser Eddie. Everyone here does. But if you wish an escort out of the marsh, I will have Saaya escort you safely to our borders. We have met so many times you and me. All I ask is for you to remember my name.'

Ser Eddie had plunged forward several steps, and the water was now up to his chest. He remembered what the yogini had said, like him, everyone here had two names.

'How many guesses do I get?'

The Mother of the Marsh giggled, 'Why how many do you want?'

The water was now at Ser Eddie's collar bones, he had little time so began shouting, 'Ammi! Amma! Ammu! Mother! Momma! Umma!'

'Oh, baby Eadwayne, not every woman is your mother,' the Mother of the Marsh hinted as she floated over to Ser Eddie.

Ser Eddie leaned his face back, the next step he took would put the water above his chin. The Mother of the Marsh leaned over slightly and Ser Eddie saw that her hair was not hair at all but snakes.

'I'm sorry I don't remember your name,' Ser Eddie cried, 'I'll do anything. Tell me.'

'That's the problem,' the Mother of the Marsh countered, 'You'll do anything, and you don't even know why.'

The Mother of the Marsh held Ser Eddie after the first snake had plunged her fangs into his neck.

The animals joined them in the water as the snakes drained Eadwayne's life source. The Mother of the Marsh carried him out of the water and asked for Saaya's blessing.

Saaya walked with the Mother of the Marsh as she carried Ser Eadwayne's body out of the stepwell. The animals followed, each returning to their own homes. Sam and Moonu stayed behind, as they walked through the stone pavilion, they heard Eadwayne's life force return. Eadwayne had found his way back to the stepwell and was whistling his tune.

Sam and Moonu joined him, watching the tiny bouncing light sparking each torch in the stone creation. Eadwayne's tune slowed and echoed as he traveled through the stepwell in his new form, the Blood Moon above them.

89: Then

Faith had brought Ana a box, which was much too large for her few belongings. Ana was surprised at how much she had collected in just a few weeks. Two of the sales reps sheepishly escorted Ana down the stairs to the main entrance. Mr. Paisley had been nice enough to offer to pay for a cab, knowing she walked to and from work every day and it would be difficult to do so carrying a heavy box.

Ana felt the sales reps eyes on her as she stood outside in the cold waiting for the cab. After she set the box down at her feet, she pushed both hands into her pockets, checking again to make sure the note she had scribbled was still there.

Ana wanted to look back over her shoulder, will the sales reps to get Faith and Raven, to tell them Willard had fired her, so they could have a last goodbye. They'd find the news out from Wayne and Willard, maybe Gabby if she wasn't fired too. Ana watched the cab pull into the parking lot and took a deep breath to prevent the tears from leaking down her face. On Ana's exhale she heard the footsteps running her way.

She turned and saw Faith and Raven. The three women embraced in a hug and Ana slipped the note from her coat pocket into Raven's hand when she squeezed it goodbye. The cab ride would only a few minutes long and she refused to look back to the offices of WWW.

When Raven got back to her office, she shut the door and stood behind it to make sure no one could see her open Ana's note up. She saw Ana had scribbled her phone number down and read the note twice before walking briskly to Gabby, navigating to the stairs leading to the Executive Suite.

Tell Gabby to blame me. <u>Do not let her quit!</u> Please read about Rufus in today's paper. I have the money to help but I don't know how any of this works. <u>PLEASE CALL ME.</u>

90: When

Prem waved as Riley rode her bike away from their cottage, promising taxi service when she got back from her shift at the clinic, she'd be waiting at Riley's parking spot with the tandem bicycle in the evening. In just a few minutes Riley was out of sight and Prem returned to their new home.

She sat down at their kitchen table, for it was also her desk, and opened up her notebook. She searched through the pocket folder and flipped through her copies of the photos, stopping to examine the ones with the curious orb of light. She pulled the business card out and dialed the number on their corded phone. Prem had insisted the cordless model be returned to Riley's mom.

Prem listened to the sounds through the phone's receiver as she drew a design of vines and flowers and snakes, the crest of Mirror Marsh in her notebook. She was polite to the receptionist, who had apologized, flustered when she answered the phone, confused at Prem's inquiry about her stone's inscription. The receptionist explained she was feeling spread thin, a little overwhelmed with her boss asking her to help the team, assigning her assistant duties to multiple engineers.

Prem was gentle with the receptionist, telling her there was no need to apologize. The line went silent until Prem spoke again, asking, "Are you okay? Are you still there?"

"Yeah, I'm sorry," the receptionist apologized again, "I'm just not used to your response. Would you let me know who you were calling for again?"

Prem read the contact information off of the business card to the receptionist and then asked her if she knew him.

"Yeah, I know him," the receptionist whispered into the phone, "He's my boss. Please don't say anything."

"I promise, I won't," Prem promised before relaying her message, asking the lead engineer for Mirror Marsh to call her back.

After she hung up Prem chose to return to her breath. To let go of her anger at how the receptionist was being treated, to forget what had happened to Manasa. She jumped when the phone rang, disturbing her peace, the silence.

"It's me again. My boss gave me the run down on your project, I'll be helping. He said to start with the inscription, do you have it ready? Then we'll move to design," the receptionist rushed, "Oh, so sorry, please hold, I have to get this."

Prem did not like the music that played when she was left on hold and set the phone back on the receiver. She tidied the kitchen and got ready for her walk to the stepwell, grabbing her notebook and shoving it in her vest.

Prem walked through the stepwell, noticing again how the snakes Manasa had chosen were all so docile, at most a forked tongue escaped their lips. Prem felt the heat of the stone on her skin as she sat on the top step, the water seemed low today and Prem knew it would only be getting lower. The sounds of the stepwell were interrupted as a rattle echoed through the stone chamber of the platform above.

Prem knew from the sun in the sky it was time to head back. Before she rode the tandem to Riley's parking spot she returned the receptionist's call. She learned her name, Mia, and shared the idea for the inscription.

Mia interrupted to clarify, "Pardon?"

Prem commanded Manasa's authority as she repeated the inscription, thinking of how much of her past was left to shed.

Prem thanked Mia before hanging up and daydreamed about her day in the city when she stopped by their firm to see their presentation of the memorial stone, possible designs she would want to honor Manasa as she walked to their tandem. It was early enough that she'd have time to take the long way, leaning the cycle against their oak. As she hopped onto the front seat she noticed something in the wicker basket at the front of her handlebars.

Prem leaned forward and smiled at the sign of good luck. She looked at the skin on the back of her hands as her palms pressed into the handlebars, they were dry but no longer uncomfortable, itchy. She looked at her veins, snaking under her thin, new skin. Prem found her balance and began pedaling, every so often looking at the basket to make sure the molted snakeskin was really there in the basket, excited to show Riley.

91: Now

Just as a serpent sheds her skin, we must shed our past again and again to make way for our new selves.

Jani read the stone before Drishti took her wax paper and charcoal to it, ready to make a copy.

"Is it safe to drink?" Jani asked as she looked over the water.

"The marsh purifies quite a bit and there's an ancient belief that your Surya was the great purifier of water. We've learned otherwise since then. It's safe to gather," Jeff Uncle said as he stood, gesturing for her to follow, "We'll boil it at home. Filter it."

Prem handed Jani the smallest copper pot there was, dark and clean. It wouldn't be too heavy when full. Jani thought on how she'd been afraid of her, worried about relying on Jeff Uncle and his machete. Drishti had explained as she had shown Jani the memorial stone for Manasa. That Prem had commissioned it for the protectress of Mirror Marsh.

Jani bent on all fours, ready to dip the pot when she noticed a common garter snake slither past her, towards the room with all of the pots Prem had stepped out from.

"It'll be alright," Drishti called to Jani, watching her as she scribbled across the stone.

"Mother Earth is our home and provides for us," Jani repeated the inscription Prem had pointed out to her as another garter snake slithered past her. Jani pushed away from the stone floor to sit back on her heels and dipped the copper pot into the water of the stepwell.

Acknowledgements

I don't quite have words for the gratitude I hold, from the depths of my heart, to my friends who have understood my anger and held it with me. When the decision was leaked, I did what I do, I wrote, and that often means those who love me receive less of my presence.

Thank you, AJ, for fighting and the good you do with your important work. May you never be asked to refill the soup when on-call, in the doctor's lounge, ever again.

B, thank you for encouraging me to write, providing all the support, and listening to me talk about snakes. A lot. You're the one I laugh with, live for, love.

JPS, thank you for always believing in me. I'm so lucky you're my friend. Again, I don't have the words. Thank you for always helping me.

CT, I love you so much. I am in awe of your friendship.

SS: you, me, & a tree; whaddya think?

Thank you HMH for always seeing me & understanding why I wanna be in 1993.

LSC, thank you for being my person. I'm proud of us for surviving & thriving in those places we can.

MH, thank you for sharing your wisdoms with me. I continue to feed two kittens with one bowl of milk & charging towards lifelines.

Thank you, PM, for being my friend since our LA days & for always being willing to talk about watersheds & hydrology. I almost forgot to acknowledge the 2,4,6,8 days. It has certainly been a trip around the isthmus.

Thank you, JT, for being so ding-dang thoughtful & for supporting my dream. Your friendship means so much.

Dear SJ, we met on IG, but I hope we can meet IRL one day. Thank you so much for reaching out & connecting with me.

M, you're an IG friend who I hope to meet IRL one day too. Thank you so much for supporting my writing & for providing your thoughts on it. Keep on doodlin'.

SZ & MM, thank you for being my friends.

MH, thanks for always hiking and wanting to do outdoor things with me. I also really appreciate how you point interesting things out to me, like certain squirrels.

SJ, thank you for inviting me into your home & for always including me. It's so special to me that you have read my books. You mean so much to me. Thank you.

Thank you, beloved reader. May you & all beings know what it is to feel loved, protected, & safe.